Lucy was drowning in raw sensation. Lying in the arms of a total stranger, drowning in the quicksilver heat of his eyes, his touch, parting her lips to gasp in air, struggling to breathe.

What was she thinking? What was she doing?

On some distant level she knew she had to move, run, but here, now, only the most primitive sensations were getting through....

She squirmed away from him in alarm, using her hands and feet to scrabble backward.

"No!"

It was the cry of a man bereft.

"Stop!"

But the urgency of Nathaniel's words spurred her on. She dodged through moving shoppers and took the stairs two at a time, fear driving her escape.

Nathaniel forced himself to move, pick up the shoe that had tumbled unnoticed from her bag.

He turned it in his hand.

It bore an expensive, high-end designer label at odds with the damp edge around the platform sole, splashes of pavement dirt on the slender and very high, very slender stiletto heel. This was not a shoe for walking in the rain. It had been made to ride in limousines, to walk along red carpets, to be worn by the consorts of very rich men. The kind who employed bodyguards.

Do you like stories that are fun and flirty?

Then you'll ♥ Harlequin® Romance's new miniseries—
where love and laughter are guaranteed!

If you love romantic comedies, look for

The Fun Factor

Warm and witty stories of falling in love

**Look out for the next title in
The Fun Factor series...coming in January:**

Molly Cooper's Dream Date
by Barbara Hannay

LIZ FIELDING
Mistletoe and the Lost Stiletto

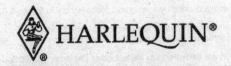

The Fun Factor

HARLEQUIN®

TORONTO • NEW YORK • LONDON
AMSTERDAM • PARIS • SYDNEY • HAMBURG
STOCKHOLM • ATHENS • TOKYO • MILAN • MADRID
PRAGUE • WARSAW • BUDAPEST • AUCKLAND

Recycling programs
for this product may
not exist in your area.

ISBN-13: 978-0-373-17696-0

MISTLETOE AND THE LOST STILETTO

First North American Publication 2010

This edition published by arrangement with Harlequin Books S.A.

For questions and comments about the quality of this book please contact us at Customer_eCare@Harlequin.ca.

® and TM are trademarks of the publisher. Trademarks indicated with ® are registered in the United States Patent and Trademark Office, the Canadian Trade Marks Office and in other countries.

www.eHarlequin.com

Printed in U.S.A.

Liz Fielding was born with itchy feet. She made it to Zambia before her twenty-first birthday and, gathering her own special hero and a couple of children on the way, lived in Botswana, Kenya and Bahrain—with pauses for sightseeing pretty much everywhere in between. She finally came to a full stop in a tiny Welsh village cradled by misty hills, and these days mostly lets her pen do the traveling. When she's not sorting out the lives and loves of her characters she potters in the garden, reads her favorite authors and spends a lot of time wondering *What if...?* For news of upcoming books—and to sign up for her occasional newsletter—visit Liz's website at www.lizfielding.com.

PROLOGUE

Wednesday, 1st December
Appointments for Miss Lucy Bright
09:30 Beauty salon
12:30 Lunch with Marji Hayes, editor, Celebrity
magazine
14:30 Celebrity photoshoot (with my mum!)
16:00 Serafina March, Wedding Designer.
20:00 Dinner at Ritz, guest list attached

Lucy Bright diary entry, 1st December:
Wish I could be at press conference for the unveiling of the Lucy B fashion chain this afternoon but, according to Rupert's dragon of a secretary, it's for the financial rather than the gossip pages. Which put me in my place. I can't even appeal to Rupert since he won't be flying in until lunchtime. And how come he gets out of the meeting with the über scary Serafina March? It's his wedding, too.

Stupid question. He's too busy for 'girl' stuff. He's been out of the country more than he's been in it for the last month and at this rate I'll be walking up the aisle on my own.

The celebration dinner tonight is, as I'm constantly reminded, my moment in the sun and, obviously,

*a morning being pampered, a luscious lunch with
the editor of* Celebrity *and then a meeting with the
wedding designer to the stars meets all the criteria
for the fairy tale. I am Lucy Bright. It's my name—
Lucy B—that's going to be above the doors of a
hundred High Street shops come the spring. So why
do I feel as if I'm on the outside looking in?*

RUBBING at the base of her engagement ring with her thumb
so that the huge diamond sparkled, Lucy Bright made an
effort to shake off the feeling that things weren't quite as
fairy tale as media coverage of her romance with Rupert
Henshawe would suggest. Determined to shake off the feeling, she logged into Twitter to update her followers on what
she'd be doing for the rest of the day.

*Morning, tweeps! Off to have the curls flattened.
Again. I swear everyone hides when I turn up at the
salon! #Cinderella*
LucyB, Wed 1 Dec 08:22

*Hair straight for the moment. Fab lunch at Ivy. Lots
of celebs. Off to meet Mum for photoshoot. Will
update blog later. #Cinderella*
LucyB, Wed 1 Dec 14:16

*PS Don't miss Rupert's Lucy B press launch live on
website feed today, tweeps! 4 p.m. It's going to be
so exciting. #Cinderella.*
LucyB, Wed 1 Dec 14:18

'Is that the time?' Lucy squeaked.
'We are running a little late, miss.' Rupert's chauffeur

held the umbrella aloft as she ran from the photoshoot to the car.

Little was an understatement. The photographer had been relentless in pursuit of the perfect photograph and she had less than twenty minutes to make the meeting with the wedding planner—sorry, make that wedding *designer*—to discuss a theme for the big day. While it was acceptable, even necessary, for the bride to arrive late at her wedding, Serafina March did not allow the same latitude where appointments with her were concerned.

'There's no time to go home for the wedding file, Gordon. We'll have to stop by the office.' Rupert's deadly efficient PA maintained a duplicate in the office. She could borrow that.

CHAPTER ONE

'LIAR!'

The only sound in the room was the clatter of motor drives as tycoon, Rupert—just-call-me-Prince-Charming—Henshawe's press conference was hijacked by his fiancée, Lucy—I-feel-like-Cinderella—Bright as she tugged off her engagement ring and flung it at him.

'Cheat!'

Every lens in the room zoomed in on the bright splash of blood where the huge diamond found its mark on Henshawe's cheek.

The gathered press pack—city newsmen, financial pundits, television news teams—held their collective breath.

They'd been summoned to a full dress press conference by the Henshawe Corporation. Whatever Henshawe did was news. Good news if you were one of his shareholders. Bad news if you happened to be on the receiving end of one of his corporate raids. At least until recently.

The news now was all about how he'd changed. How, having met his 'Cinderella', he had been redeemed by love and was no longer Mr Nasty, but had been transformed into Prince Charming.

Boring.

This was much more like it.

'Why?' Lucy demanded, ignoring the cameras, the

mikes, dangled overhead, pushed towards her face. The larger than life-sized images of herself, wearing her own custom-made originals of the Lucy B fashions, being flashed across a screen. All she could see was the man on the podium. 'Why did you do it?'

Stupid question. It was all there in the file she'd found. The one she was never meant to see. All laid out in black and white.

'Lucy! Darling…' Rupert's voice was deceptively soft as, using the power of the microphone in front of him, he drowned out her demand to know *why her?* 'These are busy people and they've got deadlines to meet. They've come to listen to the plans I've been making, *we've* been making, for the future of the company,' he stressed. 'Not a domestic tiff.'

His smile was tender, all concern for her. It was familiar, reassuring and even now it would be so easy to be sucked in…

'I don't know what's upset you but it's obvious that you're tired. Let Gordon take you home and we'll talk about it later, hmm?'

She had to fight the almost hypnotic softness of his voice. Her own weakness. Her longing for the fairy tale that had overtaken her life, transformed her into a celebrity, to be true.

She had a Lucy B fan page on Facebook, half a million people following her every word on Twitter. She was a modern day Cinderella, whisked from the hearth to a palace, her rags replaced with silken gowns. But Prince Charming's 'bride ball' had been a palace-generated crowd-pleaser, too. There was nothing like a royal wedding to keep the masses happy.

It was exactly the kind of stunt to appeal to some super-smart PR woman with a name to make for herself.

'Talk!' she hurled back as someone obligingly stuck a microphone in front of her, giving her equal voice power. 'I don't want to talk to you, Rupert Henshawe! I never even want to see you again.' She held up the file for him to see. So that he would know that there was no point in denying it. 'I know what you've done. I know *everything!*'

Even as the words left her mouth, Lucy sensed the mood in the room change. No one was looking at the podium now. Or Rupert. She'd stolen his limelight. She'd stormed into this plush hotel, her head exploding with the discovery that her new and exciting life, their engagement, the whole shooting match, was nothing more than a brilliantly executed marketing plan. The focus was now on her as she put an end to a sham smoke-and-mirrors engagement that was as false as his 'new man' change of heart.

Rupert Henshawe had no heart.

But, as the attention of the room shifted to her, it belatedly occurred to Lucy that this might not have been her best move.

In the months following her whirlwind romance with her billionaire boss she had become used to the press, but this was different. Until now she'd been supported every step of the way, whether the interviews had been personal or about her new role as the face, and name, on his re-branded chain of fashion stores.

When she'd gate-crashed this press conference, she hadn't had a thought in her but to confront the man who had so shamelessly used her.

Now the focus point of every lens, every eye in the room, she suddenly felt alone, vulnerable and all she wanted to do was escape. Escape from the lies, the cameras, the microphones. Disappear. But, as she stepped back, attempting to distance herself from Rupert, from everyone, she stumbled over someone's foot.

She put out a hand to stop herself from falling, grabbing at someone's lapel. There was the ominous sound of cloth ripping and, as she turned, instinctively, to apologise, she discovered that her retreat was blocked by a wall of bodies.

And the man whose lapel she was clinging to was now hanging onto her, pulling her towards him, shouting something into her ear as she was jostled, pushed by other newsmen trying to get closer, photographers shouting to attract her attention.

She forgot all about apologising, instead yanking her arm free. Someone tried to grab the file she was carrying. She used it to beat him off, swinging the tote bag she was carrying to clear a space, provoking a blinding series of flashes as the photographers caught the action.

Another hand made a grab for her in the scrum, catching the back of her coat. One of the buttons flew off and she nearly went down again, but the sight of two of Rupert's bodyguards elbowing aside journalists and cameramen alike as they made their way towards her sent a shot of adrenalin surging through her veins.

Until now she'd only seen the gentle side of Rupert Henshawe, had believed that he was truly her Prince Charming. But she was carrying proof of just how ruthless the man could be in pursuit of his ends and he wasn't going to let her leave with that.

Of course they would make it look as if they were rescuing her from the press scrum, but denouncing him in public, on camera, had put her on the other side.

She'd seen his eyes, the truth behind the soft words, the smile, and she knew that he'd do whatever it took to keep her quiet.

Swinging her tote again in an attempt to batter her way through the enclosing wall of bodies, she managed to make a little headway but then someone grabbed her wrist, a camera lens caught her a sharp blow on the temple and, head spinning, she staggered back.

There was a yelp loud enough to be heard over the bedlam as her stiletto heel encountered something soft and yielding.

As the man behind her backed off, swearing creatively, an apology was the furthest thing from her mind. A gap opened up and she didn't hesitate. She dived through it.

Christmas.

'Twas the season to make money.

Nathaniel Hart paused at the brushed stainless steel rail of the department store founded two hundred years earlier by another Nathaniel Hart, looking back down into the swirling mayhem of spend, spend, spend.

It was a scene being replicated in Hastings & Hart stores in major cities throughout the country as money was poured out on those small luxury items that made such easy and portable gifts. Scent, jewellery, silk scarves, all perfectly placed on the ground floor to be within easy reach for the desperate shop-and-run male.

Women, fortunately, were prepared to put real effort into shopping. They thronged the glass escalators that rose into the atrium as if ascending to the sky. An architectural illusion created by light, glass, mirrors.

He knew it was an illusion because he'd created it, just as he knew it to be a cage. One he was trapped inside.

Lucy's shoulder hurt where she'd charged the emergency exit, setting off a barrage of alarms that lent wind to her heels as she raced down the narrow, darkening streets behind the hotel.

She had no idea where she was heading, only that there

were men on her heels, all of them wanting her, all of them with their own agendas. But she was done with being used.

'Aaargh!' She let out a wail of fury as her heel caught and snapped in a grating, bringing her up with a painful jerk. Someone yelled behind her, closing fast, and she paused only long enough to kick her foot free of the grating, leaving the shoe behind, and race on, casting around desperately for a cruising cab. But there was never one when you were desperate!

Idiot, idiot, idiot...

The words hammered in her head in time to the jarring of her feet on the freezing wet pavement as she ran, dot-and-carry-one lopsidedly on one heel.

She'd just made the biggest mistake of her life. Make that the second biggest. She'd made the first when she'd fallen into the fairy tale trap.

In retrospect, she could see that calling her erstwhile Prince Charming a liar and cheat in front of the nation's assembled press pack had not been her brightest move. But what was a girl to do when her magic castle-in-the-air had just turned into one of those blow-up bouncy things they had at kids' parties?

Stop and think?

Stand back, line up her allies before firing her ammunition from a safe distance? Hardly the action of the girl Rupert had proclaimed to love for her spontaneity, her passion.

That was the difference between them.

The woman who'd appeared on the cover of *Celebrity* wasn't some figment of a PR man's imagination. She was real. Capable of feeling not just joy but pain. Which was why she'd leapt in with both feet, puncturing the fake castle with the four-inch heels of her Louboutins, letting out the hot air and bringing it down around her.

Idiot was right but who, having just discovered that she was the victim of the most cynical, manipulative, emotional fraud imaginable, would be thinking *rationally?*

As for allies, there was no one she could turn to. The press had already bought everyone who'd known her since she was a baby—anyone who had a photograph or a story to tell. Every moment of her life was now public property and what they didn't know they'd made up.

And Rupert owned the rest.

All those people who had fawned over her, pretended to be her friend, there wasn't one she could trust or be sure was genuine rather than someone on his PR company's payroll.

As for her mother...

She had no one and, run as hard as she might, nowhere to go. Her legs were buckling beneath her, lungs straining as she headed instinctively for the sparkle of Christmas lights and crowds of shoppers in which to lose herself, but she couldn't stop.

In moments her pursuers would be on her and she didn't need the dropping temperature, the huge white flakes that had begun to swirl from a leaden sky, to send a shiver up her spine. Then, as she rounded a corner seeking the safety of the crowds of Christmas shoppers, she saw the soaring asymmetrical glass pyramid of Hastings & Hart lighting up the winter gloom like a beacon.

She'd been in the store just the day before on a mission from Rupert to choose luscious Christmas gifts for his staff. Giving the gossip mag photographers who followed her everywhere their photo opportunities. It was all there in the files.

The plan to keep her fully occupied. Too busy to think.

The store seemed to mock her now and yet inside were nine warm and welcoming floors, each offering a hundred places to hide. Within its walls she would be off the street, safe for a while, and she flew across the street, dodging through the snarled-up traffic, heading towards the main entrance, slithering to a halt as she saw the doorman guarding the entrance.

Only yesterday he'd tipped his top hat to her in deference to her chauffeur-driven status.

He wouldn't be so impressed by her arrival today but, dishevelled and limping, he would certainly remember her and, pulling her coat tidily around her and shouldering her bag, she teetered precariously on her bare toe as she slowed down to saunter past him, doing her best to look as if she was out for a little shopping.

'You'll find footwear on the ground floor, ma'am,' he said, face absolutely straight, as he opened the door. And tipped his hat.

Scanning the ground floor from his bird's-eye view, Nat's attention was caught by two burly men in dark suits who'd paused in the entrance. They were looking about them, but not in the baffled, slightly desperate way of men trying to decide what gift would make their Christmas a memorable one.

Men didn't shop in pairs and he could tell at a glance that these two weren't here to pick out scents for the women in their life.

He'd seen the type often enough to recognise them as either close protection officers or bodyguards.

The doorman, well used to welcoming anyone from a royal to a pop star, would have alerted the store's security staff to the arrival of a celebrity, but curiosity held him for the moment, interested to see who would follow them through the doors.

No one.

At least no one requiring a bodyguard, just the usual stream of visitors to the store, excited or harassed, who broke around the pair and joined the throng in the main hall.

Frowning now, he remained where he was, watching as the two men exchanged a word, then split up and began to work their way around the glittering counters, eyes everywhere, clearly looking for someone.

Make that a charge who had given her bodyguards the slip.

In the main hall, mobbed in the run-up to Christmas as shoppers desperately tried to tick names off their gift lists and stocked up on exotic, once-a-year luxuries, Lucy had hoped that no one would notice her. That once she was inside the store she'd be safe.

She'd been fooling herself.

She did her best to style it out, but she hadn't fooled the doorman and several people turned to look as she tried—and failed—to keep herself on an even keel. And then looked again, trying to think where they'd seen her before.

The answer was everywhere.

Rupert was *Celebrity* magazine's new best friend and his and her—mostly her—faces had been plastered over it for weeks. Their romance was news and cameras had followed her every move.

Everything she'd done, everywhere she'd been was a story and, as she tried to ease through the crowd, eyes down, she knew she was being stared at.

Then, from somewhere at the bottom of her bag, her phone began to belt out her *I'm In Love With a Wonderful Guy* ringtone.

Could anything be any less appropriate?

Or loud.

She might as well put a great big sign over her head, lit up and flashing 'Dumb blonde here!'

Hampered by the file, she hunted for the wretched thing but, by the time she'd dug it out of the bottom of the bag, it had gone to voicemail. Not for the first time.

There had been half a dozen missed calls while she'd been making her escape and, as she looked at it, it beeped at her, warning that she now had a text, adding to her sense of being hunted.

She had to get off the ground floor and out of sight—now—and, giving up on the attempt to look casual, she kicked off her remaining shoe—after all, if she was four inches shorter she'd be less noticeable—and stuffed it, along with the file, in her bag.

As far as she could recall, the nearest powder room was on the third floor. If she made that without being discovered, she could hole up there for a while, lock herself in a cubicle and think. Something she should have done before barging into that press conference.

Avoiding the glass lifts and escalators—her red coat was too bright, too noticeable and the people following her had been close enough, smart enough to have figured out where she'd gone to earth—she hurried towards the stairs.

It was a good plan. The only problem with it was that by the time she'd reached the first floor she had a stitch in her side, her legs felt like jelly and her head was swimming from the crack on the temple.

For a moment she bent double as she tried to ease the pain.

'Are you all right?' A sweet lady was looking at her with concern.

'Fine,' she lied. 'Just a stitch.' But the minute the woman was out of sight she slithered behind a floor-to-ceiling arrangement of silver and white snowflakes that had been constructed in the corner where the stairs turned. Safely out of sight, she sank down onto the floor and used her free hand to massage her ankles, which were aching from the strain. She pulled a face as she saw the state of her foot. Her shredded tights. But there was nothing she could do about that now.

Instead, she leaned back against the wall to catch her breath, regarding the state-of-the-art all-singing, all-dancing phone that had so quickly become a part of her new life with uncertainty.

It held all her contacts, appointments. She dictated her thoughts into it. Her private diary. The elation, the disbelief, the occasional doubt. And it was her connection to a world that seemed endlessly fascinated by her.

Her Facebook page, the YouTube videos, her Twitter account.

Rupert's PR people hadn't been happy when they'd discovered that she'd signed up to Twitter all by herself. Actually, it had been her hairdresser who'd told her that she was being tweeted about and showed her how to set up her own account while waiting for her highlights to take.

That had been the first warning that she wasn't supposed to have a mind of her own, but keep to the script.

Once they'd realised how well it was working, though, they'd encouraged her to tweet her every thought, every action, using the Cinderella hashtag, to her hundreds of thousands of followers. Keep them up to date with her transformation from Cinderella into Rupert's fairy tale princess.

Innocently selling the illusion. Doing their dirty work for them.

But it was a two-way thing.

Right now her in-box was filling up with messages from followers who had watched the web feed, seen the ruckus and, despite everything, she smiled as she read them.

@*LucyB* Nice bag work, Cinders! What's occurring? #Cinderella
WelshWitch, [+] Wed 1 Dec 16:08

@*LucyB* What's the b*****d done, sweetie? #Cinderella
jenpb, [+] Wed 1 Dec 16:09

@*LucyB* DM me a contact number. You're going to need help. #Cinderella
prguru, [+] Wed 1 Dec 16:12

Too true, she thought, the smile fading. But not from 'prguru', aka Mr Public Relations, the man famous for selling grubby secrets to grubby newspapers and gossip mags. It didn't matter to him if you were a model in rehab, a politician having an affair with his PA or the victim of some terrible tragedy. He'd sell your story for hard cash and turn you into a celebrity overnight.

Nor any of the other public relations types lining up to jump in and feed off her story. As if she'd trust anyone in the PR business ever again.

She wasn't sure how long the phone would function—Rupert would surely pull the plug the minute he thought of it—so she quickly thumbed in a message to her followers while she had the chance.

And maybe she should update her diary, too. Just in case

anything happened to her. Something else her hairdresser had clued her up on. That she could set up a private web document, record her thoughts on her phone and then send it to be stored on her own private Internet space.

'Think of it as your pension, princess,' he'd said.

She'd thought him cynical, but she had started keeping a diary, mostly because there were some things she hadn't been able to confide to anyone else.

Diary update: *Day hit the skids after the photoshoot when I realised I'd forgotten the wedding file and went to the office to borrow R's copy. His dragon of a personal assistant had gone with him to the Lucy B press launch and her assistant is on holiday so there was a temp holding the fort or I would never have been handed the key to his private filing cabinet.*

I had my hand on the wedding file when I spotted the one next to it. The one labelled 'The Cinderella Project'.

Well, of course I opened it. Wouldn't you?

Now meeting with wedding planner off. Celebration off. Dinner at Ritz most definitely off. As for wedding... Off, off, off.

Time to Tweet the good news.

Thanks for concern, tweeps. Fairy tale fractured—kissed prince, got frog. HEA cancelled. End of story. #Cinderella
LucyB, [+] Wed 1 Dec 16:41

The phone belted out the ghastly ringtone again just as she clicked 'send' and made her jump nearly out of her skin. It was a sharp reminder of the need to keep her head down and she switched it to silent, unable to cut herself off entirely.

There had to be someone she could ring. Someone she could trust. But not from here.

This was no haven.

She had to move before someone spotted her, but first she had to do something to change her appearance.

She'd felt so utterly Christmassy when she'd set off in her bright red coat that morning. Utterly full of the joys of a season that had never before felt so exciting, so full of promise.

Now she felt as conspicuous as Santa in a snowdrift.

She would have liked to abandon it. Abandon everything. Strip off, change back into who she was. Her real self, not this manufactured 'princess'.

Easier said than done.

This morning she'd had everything a woman could possibly want. This afternoon she had nothing in the world except what she stood up in and it was going to be freezing tonight.

But she could manage without the coat for now and, easing it off in the cramped space, she folded it inside out so that only the black lining showed. Better, although she could have done with a hat to cover her head.

She didn't even have a scarf. Why would she? Until half an hour ago she was being chauffeured everywhere, an umbrella held over her head at the slightest suggestion of anything damp descending from the sky whenever she stepped onto a pavement. Cosseted. Precious.

Very precious. A lot of time and money had been invested in her. And Rupert—not the fantasy figure of her dreams, but the real one—would expect, demand a profit for all that effort, cost.

Legs still a little shaky, she shouldered her bag, tucked

her coat over her arm and, still clutching her phone in her hand, peered cautiously around the display.

No sign of any big scary men, or journalists, hunting her down, just shoppers preoccupied with what to wear at a Christmas party or buying gifts for their loved ones. Taking a deep breath and doing her best to look as if it was the most normal thing in the world, she eased herself back into the flow.

It took all her nerve to take one ladylike step after the other, matching her pace to those around her and trying to look as if walking barefoot through the poshest store in London in December was absolutely normal, when what she really wanted to do was take off, race up the stairs two at a time and get out of sight.

She kept her eyes straight ahead instead of looking about her to check for anything suspicious, doing absolutely nothing that might draw attention to herself.

Nat called down to his head of security to brief him on the fact that they might have a 'situation'; something to keep an eye on. That done, he continued his afternoon walk through the store, conscientiously looking in on each department before heading for the stairs to the next floor.

Even at the height of the Christmas buying frenzy the H&H reputation for perfection had to be maintained. He might not want to be here, but no one would ever be able to accuse him of letting standards slip and he was alert for anything that jarred on the eye, anything out of place.

Why, for instance, had the woman ahead of him taken off her coat? Was the store too warm? It was essential that shoppers had both hands free, but it was a delicate balancing act keeping the store comfortable for both staff and customers who were dressed for outdoors.

Not that he was complaining about the view.

She had pale blonde hair cut in soft, corn silk layers that seemed to float around her head, stirring a thousand memories. Despite the fact that they were in the middle of the busiest shopping season of the year, he wanted to slow the world down, call out her name so that she'd turn to him with an unguarded smile...

He slammed the door on the thought but, even while his brain was urging him to pass her, move on, the rest of him refused to listen, hanging back so that he could hold on to the illusion for a moment longer.

Foolish.

She was nothing like the fragile woman whose memory she'd evoked. On the contrary, the black cashmere sweater-dress she was wearing clung enticingly to a figure that curved rather more than was fashionable. No snow queen, this. Inches shorter, she was an altogether earthier armful. Not the kind of woman you worshipped from afar, but the kind built for long, dark winter nights in front of an open fire.

Then, as his gaze followed the pleasing curve of her hip to the hem of her short skirt and he found himself enjoying the fact that her legs lived up to the rest of the package, he realised that she wasn't wearing any shoes.

She might have taken them off for a moment's relief. It wouldn't be the first time he'd seen a woman walking barefoot through the store carrying shoes that were pinching after a hard day's shopping. But she wasn't laden with glossy carriers. The only bag she was carrying was a soft leather tote clutched close to her side beneath the coat, heavy, but with the weight of a protruding file rather than parcels, gift-wrapped by his staff.

But what really jarred, jolting him out of the firelight fantasy, was the fact that one foot of the ultra-fine black tights she was wearing had all but disintegrated. That her slender ankles had been splashed with dirt thrown up from the wet pavements.

As if sensing him staring, she turned, still moving, and almost in slow motion he saw her foot miss the step and she flung out her arm, grabbing for him as she stumbled backwards.

He caught her before she hit the stairs and for a moment they seemed to hang there, suspended above them, his hand beneath her as she peered up at him with startled kitten eyes, her arm flung around his neck.

His head filled with the jarringly familiar scent of warm skin overlaid with some subtle, expensive perfume that jumped to his senses, intensified colour, sound, touch…the softness of the cashmere, the curve of her back, her weight against his palm as he supported her, kissing close to full, soft lips, slightly parted as she caught her breath.

His world was reduced to the pounding of his heart, her breath against his cheek, her gold-green eyes peering up at him over a voluptuous cowl collar that was sliding, seductively, off one shoulder.

She smelled like a summer garden, of apples and spice and, as he held her, a rare, forgotten warmth rippled through him.

CHAPTER TWO

LUCY was drowning in raw sensation. Lying in the arms of a total stranger, drowning in the quicksilver heat of his eyes, his touch, parting her lips to gasp in air, struggling to breathe as she went under for the third time.

What was she thinking? What was she doing?

For a moment her brain, its buffer overloaded with more information, more emotion, more of just about everything than a body was built to handle, had backed up, was refusing to compute.

On some distant level she knew she had to move, run, but here, now, only the most primitive sensations were getting through. Touch, warmth, confusion...

'The bedroom department is on the fifth floor,' someone said with a chuckle as she passed and Nat felt, rather than saw the sudden realisation hit her.

The sheer madness of it. But her reaction was not the same dazed feeling that had him staring at her like an idiot. Not even an embarrassed laugh.

Instead she emitted a little squeak of alarm and squirmed away from him, using her hands and feet to scrabble backwards up the steps before she got far enough away to turn, push herself to her feet and run.

'No!'

It wasn't a command, it was the cry of a man bereft.

'Stop!'

But the urgency of his words spurred her on, giving her feet wings as she bolted, dodging through slower moving shoppers, taking the stairs two at a time, fear driving her escape.

Leaving him shaking, frozen to the spot while visitors to the store flowed around him. Not surprise, or pleasure, or even amusement at an unexpectedly close encounter with a stranger. Raw fear that dredged up the memory of another woman who'd run from his arms. Who, just for a moment, he'd forgotten.

Fear, and the bruise darkening her temple.

Someone tutted irritably at him for blocking the stairs and he forced himself to move, pick up the shoe that had tumbled, unnoticed, from her bag.

He turned it in his hand.

It bore an expensive high-end designer label at odds with the damp edge around the platform sole, splashes of pavement dirt on the slender and very high stiletto heel. This was not a shoe for walking in the rain. It had been made to ride in limousines, walk along red carpets, to be worn by the consort of a very rich man. The kind who employed bodyguards.

Could she be the one the two men on the ground floor were seeking? That might explain her fear, because she hadn't run from his touch. On the contrary, she'd been equally lost, wrapped up in a sizzling moment of discovery until a crass comment had jolted her back to reality.

He didn't know who she was or why they were looking for her, only that she was afraid, running perhaps for her life, and the last thing he wanted was to draw more attention to her. No one hunted a frightened woman in his store, not even him, and he clamped down on the swamping need to race after her, reassure her, know her.

Not that there was any need to hunt.

If she was looking for a hiding place, common sense suggested that she was heading for the nearest Ladies cloakroom, looking for somewhere to clean up, hide out for a while.

But why?

His jaw tightened as he continued up the stairs with rather more speed, fighting to hold back the memories of another frightened woman. Vowing to himself that, whoever she was, she'd find sanctuary within his walls. That history wouldn't repeat itself.

He'd ask one of the senior floor managers to check on her, return her shoe, offer whatever assistance she felt appropriate. A new pair of tights with the compliments of the store. A discreet exit. A car, if necessary, to take her wherever she needed to go.

But his hand was shaking as he called Security again, wanting to know where the two men were now.

Before he could speak, he was practically knocked off his feet by one of them, racing up the stairs, heedless of the safety of the women and children in his way, running through, rather than around them, scattering bags, toys.

His first reaction was to go after him, toss him bodily out of the store, but a child was crying and he had no choice but to stop and ensure that no one was hurt, pick up scattered belongings and summon one of his staff to offer the courtesy of afternoon tea in the Garden Restaurant. Deal with the complaints before they were voiced. It was a point of honour that no one left Hastings & Hart unhappy.

But, all the time he was doing that, the questions were pounding at his brain.

Whose bodyguards? Who was her husband, lover? More to the point, who was she?

And why was she so scared?

While her face—what had been visible over the big, enveloping collar—had seemed vaguely familiar, she wasn't some instantly recognizable celebrity or minor royal. If she had been, her bodyguards wouldn't have wasted time scouring the store for her but would have gone straight to his security staff to enlist their help using CCTV. Keeping it low-key. No drama.

There was something very wrong about this and, moving with considerably more urgency now, he ordered Security to find and remove the two men from the store. He didn't care who they worked for, or who they'd lost, they had worn out their welcome.

'Hold the lift!' Lucy, trembling more now than when she'd run from the press conference, heart pounding beyond anything she'd ever experienced, sprinted for the closing doors. 'Thanks,' she gasped as someone held them and she dived in, squeezing into a corner, her back to the door where she wouldn't be instantly visible when they opened again. Her brain working logically on one level, while everything else was saying, no... Go back...

'Doors closing. Going down...'

She snapped out of the mental dream state in which she was floating above the stairs, her whole world contained in a stranger's eyes.

Nooooo! Up, up...

The recorded announcement listed the departments as, despairing, she was carried back down to the ground floor. *'Perfumery, accessories, leather goods, stationery. Ground floor. Doors opening.'*

As the doors slid open, she risked a glance, then froze as she caught sight of one of Rupert's bodyguards scanning the surge of passengers making a beeline for the exit.

She pressed herself back into the corner of the lift,

keeping her head down, drawing a curious glance from a child who looked up at her as the lift rapidly filled. Holding her breath until the doors finally closed, aware that it wasn't just the people she recognized who would be searching for her.

She'd got used to the front page—she'd been booked for a photoshoot this afternoon just to show off her new haircut, for heaven's sake—but this was different.

She'd announced to the world that she had the goods on Rupert Henshawe and it wouldn't be just the gossip magazines who'd want to know where she was.

Within hours there would be a press-orchestrated manhunt. It was probably already underway. And there was the risk that any minute now someone was going to say Excuse me, but aren't you, Lucy B?

It had happened before when she'd been shopping and the result tended to be mayhem. It was as if everyone wanted to touch her, capture a little of the magic.

Rupert's marketing men had got that right, but it was the last thing she wanted now so she kept her head tucked well down, desperate not to catch anyone's eye.

Not all eyes were over five feet from the ground, however, and she found herself being scrutinised by the little girl, who continued to stare at her as the recorded announcement said, 'Going down... *Sporting goods, gardening and recreation, electrical. And...*' there was a pause. '...*The North Pole...*'

The rest was drowned out by whoops of excitement.

'Are you going to see Santa?' the child asked her as the doors closed.

Santa?

Well, that explained why the North Pole had been relocated to a department store basement.

'We're going on a sleigh ride to see him at the North Pole,' she confided.

'Well, golly… What a treat.'

Right now a sleigh ride to the North Pole was exactly what she could do with. She'd planned to clean herself up, certain she'd be safe for a while in the Ladies. She didn't know what had made her look back. Just a feeling, a prickle on the back of her neck…

The man following her hadn't been a bodyguard. She knew them all and that wasn't a face she would have forgotten.

Eyes grey as granite, with just a spark of silver to lighten an overall sense of darkness; a reflection from the store's silver and white decorations, no doubt. That moment of magic was all in her imagination. It had to be. Whoever he was, he'd oozed the kind of power and arrogance she'd come to associate with Rupert's most intimate circle.

He was a power broker, the kind of man who took orders rather than giving them. She'd learned to recognise the type. Mostly they ignored her and she was happy about that, but there had been an intensity in his look as he'd caught her, held her, that had turned her bones to putty. And not with fear.

A déjà vu moment if ever there was one, the difference being that whatever Rupert had been feeling on the day he'd picked her up, dusted her off, all concern and charm, her heart rate hadn't gone through the roof. The air hadn't crackled, sizzled, fried her brains. He'd taken his time, wooed her so gently, so…so damn *sweetly* that she'd fallen for every scummy lie. Hook, link and sinker.

She'd thought he was the genuine article, a real Prince Charming, when the truth was he hadn't actually fancied her enough to jump her bones.

The grey-eyed stranger, on the other hand, had made

her forget everything with a look. It was as if his touch had fired up some deep, untapped sexual charge and she felt her skin flush with heat from head to toe at the memory, the promise of the kiss that she'd been waiting for all her life. The real thing.

Maybe.

She shivered. Shook her head. She'd been drawn into a web of lies and deceit and she would never be able to trust anyone ever again. Never be able to take anyone at face value.

Mortified as she'd been at being discovered as good as kissing a total stranger on the stairs, that remark had jolted her back to reality. Common sense and self-preservation had kicked in and she'd run because there were some mistakes a smart woman didn't make twice.

Some she didn't make once.

She'd thought the Ladies room would provide a safe haven but, even as she'd bolted, she'd realised her mistake. It would be obvious to anyone with half a brain cell that was where she'd take cover and in the nick of time she'd seen the trap. That it was a dead end with only one exit.

It was several hours until the store closed, but Rupert was a patient man. He'd wait, call up female reinforcements to keep an eye on her until she had no choice but to emerge.

He had enough of them.

All those women in his office who'd collaborated with him in the make-believe.

What she needed was somewhere to hide, a bolt-hole where no one would ever think of looking for her while she considered her options. Easier said than done.

All she possessed in the world was what she currently wore. She'd been too shocked to plan anything. To even think of going back to the little apartment at the top of

Rupert's London house. Packing the gorgeous wardrobe that was all part of the fantasy. Always supposing she'd got out with a suitcase.

No doubt someone would have delayed her while the alarm was raised and Rupert was warned that the game was up.

And she'd bet the farm that the platinum credit cards Rupert had showered on her would go *uh-uh* if she attempted to use them.

Or maybe not. Could he use them to track her movements? Or was that just something they did in TV thrillers?

Either way, they were useless. Not that she wanted anything from him. Right now she wished she could rip off the clothes she was wearing and toss them in the nearest bin.

Since she was trying not to draw attention to herself, that probably wasn't her best option.

Not that she'd done such a good job of keeping a low profile, she thought, still aware of the tingling imprint of a stranger's kiss.

'Do you think there'll be room on the sleigh for me?' she asked the little girl.

She lifted her shoulders in a don't-know shrug, then said, 'Do you believe in Santa Claus?'

Tough question. Right now, she was having trouble believing that the sky was blue.

'My big sister said there's no such person,' she added, then stuck her thumb in her mouth, clearly afraid that it might be true.

Okay, not that tough.

In her years working in the day-care nursery, she'd come across this one plenty of times. Big sisters could be the pits, although right now she wished she had one. A really cynical, know-it-all big sister who would have ripped away the rose-tinted spectacles, shattered her naivety, said, *Prince Charming? Are you kidding? What are the odds?*

She wasn't about to let that happen for this little girl, though. Not yet.

'Your sister only told you that because she thinks that if you don't write to Santa she'll get more presents.'

The thumb popped out. 'Really?'

Before she could reply, the lift came to a halt and the doors opened, sending her heart racing up into her mouth. Under cover of the mothers, dads, children pouring out, she risked a glance.

There were no dark-eyed men lying in wait for her, only more parents with hyped-up children, clutching gifts from Santa, waiting in a magical snowy landscape to be whisked back up to the real world. Which was where she'd go if she didn't make a move and get out of the lift. And that was not an appealing place right now.

Nowhere near as attractive as the North Pole, which the finger-post sticking out at an angle from a designer snowdrift suggested was somewhere to her right. As if to confirm that fact, an ornate sleigh was waiting in a glittering ice cave, ready to whisk the children away.

They stampeded towards it, climbing aboard while their mothers dealt with the more mundane matter of checking in with the elf in charge of the departure gate. Trips to the North Pole did not, after all, come cheap.

She barely hesitated.

She could do with a little magic herself right now and Santa's Grotto had to be just about the last place anyone would think of looking for her.

As she stood in the queue she nervously checked her phone—it was as good a way to keep her head down as any.

There were half a dozen texts, voicemail messages and the twittersphere had apparently gone mad. *WelshWitch* had started it with—

Where is Cinderella? What have you done to her? Tell the truth, Your Frogginess! RT@LucyB Kissed prince, got frog. #Cinderella
WelshWitch, [+] Wed 1 Dec 17:01

It had already been replied to by dozens of people. Rupert was going to be furious, but since this—unlike all her other social media stuff set up by his PR team—was her personal account, there wasn't a thing His Frogginess could do about it. At least not while she managed to stay out of his way.

What he might do if he caught up with her was something else. She shivered involuntarily as she continued to scroll through the tweets.

There was another one from Jen.

@LucyB If you need a bolt-hole, DM me. #Cinderella
jenpb, [+] Wed 1 Dec 17:03

In a moment of weakness she almost did send her a direct message. But then she came to her senses and shut the phone.

That was what was so horrible about this. It wasn't just Rupert she couldn't trust.

She'd chatted daily on Twitter. She had nearly half a million 'followers', an army of fans on Facebook, all apparently fascinated by her story, her amazing new life. But who were they really?

Jen had seemed like a genuine friend, one of a few

people who, like WelshWitch, she constantly tweeted with, but suppose she was just another of Rupert's people? Someone the PR company had delegated to stay close. Be her 'friend', guide her tweets, distract her if necessary, steer her away from anything controversial? She was well aware that not everyone in the Twittersphere was who or what they seemed. Logging into her appointments, she scrolled down and, under the crossed-through entry for *Dinner at Ritz*, she added another entry—

Rest of life: up the creek.

And then her thoughts shifted back to the man on the stairs. His face forever imprinted on her memory. The strong jaw, high cheekbones, the sensuous curve of his lower lip...

'Can I help?'

She jumped, looked up to discover that everyone else had moved off and she was being regarded by a young elf.

'Oh...um...one adult to the North Pole, please,' she said, closing her phone and reaching for her purse, wondering belatedly how much it would cost. She didn't have that much cash. With a fistful of credit and charge cards, she hadn't needed it. 'A single will do,' she said. 'I'm in no hurry. I can walk back.'

He grinned appreciatively but said, 'Sorry. This flight has closed.'

'Oh.' It hadn't occurred to her that there wouldn't be any room. 'How long until the next one?'

'Forty minutes, but you have to have a pre-booked ticket to see Santa,' he explained.

'You have to book in advance?' Forty minutes! She

couldn't wait that long. 'Where's the magic in that?' she demanded.

'There's not much magical about dozens of disappointed kids screaming their heads off,' he pointed out.

'True...' She had enough experience with screaming children not to argue. 'Look, I don't actually want to have a one-to-one with the man himself. I just need to get to the North Pole,' she pressed as the doors to the ice cave began to close. 'It's really urgent...'

It occurred to her that she must sound totally crazy. That, shoeless and apparently raving, she was going to be escorted from the premises.

It didn't happen. Apparently, someone who could cite 'elf' as his day job took crazy in his stride because, instead of summoning Security, he said, 'Oh, *right*. I was told to look out for you.'

What...? *Nooooo!*

'You're from Garlands, right? Pam's been going crazy,' he added before the frantic message from her brain to flee could reach her feet. 'She expected you ages ago.'

'Garlands...'

What the heck was that? The department responsible for store decorations? Did a snowflake need straightening? A tree trimming?

Whatever.

She was up for it, just as long as she was out of sight of the lift.

'You've got me,' she said, neither confirming nor denying it. 'So, *now* do I get a ride on the sleigh?'

'Sorry,' he said, grinning. 'The sleigh is for paying customers only. Staff have to put on their snow shoes and walk. Both ways,' he added with relish. Clearly this was a young man who enjoyed his job. 'Don't look so worried.

I'm kidding about the snow shoes.' He looked at her feet and, for a moment, lost the thread.

'It's a long story,' she said.

'Er…right. Well, you're in luck. There's a short cut.' He opened a door, hidden in the side of a snow bank and tucked behind the kind of huge Christmas tree that you only ever saw in story books. Smothered with striped candy canes, toys, beautiful vintage decorations. 'Turn left, ask for Pam Wootton. She'll sort you out.'

'Left…Pam… Got it. Thanks.'

Better and better. She'd be much safer behind the scenes in the staff area.

Forget Pam whatever-her-name-was. She'd keep her head down until closing time and then leave through the staff entrance with everyone else. By then, she might even have worked out where she could go.

'She's not in there, Mr Hart.'

'Are you sure? She hasn't locked herself in one of the cubicles?'

'All checked. That's what took me so long.'

'Well, thanks for looking,' he said, outwardly calm.

'No problem.' She hesitated, then said, 'The lifts are right opposite the stairs. If she got lucky with the timing, she might have doubled straight back down to the ground floor and left the store.'

'It's possible,' Nat agreed, although he doubted it. He had her shoe and no one with a lick of sense would choose to go barefoot from the warmth of the store into the street. She was still in the store; he was certain of it. And, with nine sales floors, she had plenty of places to hide.

In her shoes—or, rather, lack of them—where would he go? What would he do?

If it was serious—and her fear suggested that this wasn't

just some rich woman wanting a little time out—changing her appearance had to be the first priority. Not a problem when she had a store full of clothes and accessories to help her, except that would mean exposing herself while she stood in line to pay for them.

Maybe.

Just how desperate was she?

Desperate enough to grab something from a rail, switch clothes in one of the changing rooms? When they were this busy it wouldn't be that difficult and she could rip out the security tags without a second thought. It wouldn't matter to her if the clothes were damaged, only that they didn't set off the alarms when she walked out of the store.

'I'll put the shoe in Lost Property, shall I?'

'No!' Realising that he'd overreacted, that she was look-ing at him at little oddly, he said, taking the shoe from her, 'I'll do it. I've already wasted enough of your time. Thanks for your help.'

'No problem, Mr Hart. I'll keep my eyes open.'

He nodded, but doubted she'd see her and, more in hope than expectation of finding some clue, he retraced his steps back down to the first floor, where he stopped to take an-other look out over the busy ground floor.

As the afternoon had shifted into evening and offices had emptied, it had become even more frantic, but he would have spotted that black dress amid the madness, the pale blonde swish of hair. That was a real giveaway, one that she should cover up as quickly as possible.

She'd need a scarf, he thought. Or a hat. A hat would be better. It would not only cover her hair, but throw a shadow over her face where a scarf would only draw attention to it.

And once she'd changed her appearance she could risk the shoe department. He'd wait there.

As he started down the stairs, he noticed a display slightly out of alignment, stopped to adjust it and saw a lace-trimmed handkerchief lying on the floor.

He bent to pick it up and caught again that faint, subtle scent that hadn't come out of any bottle.

Had she dashed in from the street to take cover, bolted up the stairs, paused here for a moment to catch her breath, get her bearings?

Where was she now?

Famous last thoughts.

The minute Lucy opened the door to the staff area she was leapt upon by a flushed and harassed-looking woman wearing a security badge proclaiming her to be Pam Wootton, Human Resources.

'At last! The agency said you'd be here an hour ago. I'd just about given up hope.'

Agency? Oh, good grief, the elf hadn't been talking about Christmas garlands but the Garland Agency. The suppliers of the crème de la crème of secretarial staff. She'd had an interview with them when she was looking for a job but she didn't have the kind of experience it took to be a 'Garland Girl'.

There was a certain irony in being mistaken for one now, but she wasn't going to let that stop her from grabbing the opportunity with both hands.

'I'm soooo sorry. The Underground…' She didn't have to say another word. It was the excuse that just gave and gave. 'And it's started to snow,' she threw in for good measure.

'Snow! Oh, great,' Pam said. 'That's all I need. Getting home tonight is going to be a nightmare.' And she pressed her hand to her forehead as if trying to keep her brain in.

'Are you all right?' Lucy asked, forgetting her own worries for a moment. The woman looked flushed and not at all well.

'Ask me again in February,' she replied with a slightly hysterical laugh. 'When the January sales are over.' Then, pulling herself together, 'It's just a bit of a headache. I'll take something for it when I get back to the office. Come on, there's no time to waste. Let's get you changed.'

'Changed?'.

'Into your costume,' she said, opening a cupboard and revealing a rail of short green tunics. Then, glancing back at her, 'Didn't they tell you anything...' she looked at her clipboard '...I don't seem to have your name.'

'Lu...' *Noooooo!*

Pam looked up. 'Lou? As in Louise?'

Gulp.

'Yes! Louise.' Whew. Pam was still waiting. 'Louise... Braithwaite.' It was the first name that came into her head.

'And you *have* got a CRB Certificate, Louise?' Pam asked, pen poised to tick boxes, going through the motions.

'A CRB Certificate?'

She sighed. 'You can't work in the grotto without a criminal records check. I did explain the situation to Garlands. If you haven't got one...'

Grotto?

The penny dropped.

Pam had mistaken her for an elf.

Out of the fairy tale frying pan, into the...um...fairy tale fire...

CHAPTER THREE

'DIDN'T Garlands explain?' Pam asked.

'It was a bad connection...' so bad it was non-existent '...I must have missed that bit. But I have been CRB checked,' she said. 'I worked in a day-care nursery before... Well, until recently.'

Oh, boy, Lucy Bright. The ability to look someone in the eye and tell a big fat lie had to be catching. His Frogginess would be proud of her.

Not that she'd lied about having a CRB Certificate. It wasn't under the name Louise Braithwaite, of course, but it was the real deal. She'd had to have one for the day job at the nursery while she'd been studying at night school. She'd worked as a waitress in the local pizza parlour on her free evenings and at the weekends to earn the money to pay for her course.

Much good it had done her.

She'd applied for hundreds of jobs before she'd got an interview for a clerical assistant post at the Henshawe Corporation. The fact that there had been an interview panel for such a junior position had thrown her, but it had been very informal. They'd been incredibly impressed at how hard she'd worked and encouraged her to talk about her ambitions.

She still remembered the stunned silence when she'd

finished telling them passionately that she wanted to prove herself. Make something of herself, be someone. And then they'd applauded her.

When, the following day, they had called her to offer her a job, she'd thought herself the luckiest woman in the world.

'I realise that Garlands know what they're doing, but I still have to ask,' Pam muttered. 'It's been so difficult since the new laws about working with children were introduced. We normally get in drama students at Christmas but not too many of them have had the foresight to get a CRBC. I don't suppose they see themselves doing a Christmas gig as one of Santa's Little Helpers when they get a place at RADA. That's why I called Garlands.'

'They supply elves?' she asked, which got her an odd look.

'They place temporary nannies.'

'Just kidding.' *Whew...*

Pam stared down at her feet. 'What happened to your shoes?'

'I broke a heel in a grating.' The truth, the whole truth and almost nothing but the truth...

'Oh, bad luck.' They shared a moment of silent mourning, then, pressing on, 'You're a bit buxom for an elf,' she said, looking at her doubtfully, 'but beggars can't be choosers. There should be something that fits.' She held one of the tunics up against her, then thrust it at her, piling the rest of the costume on top. 'You've got small feet. These should do.' She put a pair of soft felt bootees on top of the pile and then took a small plastic pouch out of a box and added that to the pile. 'The elf make-up pack. Rouge for your cheeks, a pencil for freckles—you'll find a picture of what's required inside. And there's a pad to remove your nail polish. You can change down here,' she said, leading the way down a short flight of steps. 'Find a spare locker for your clothes and be as quick as you can.'

She opened a door and Lucy found herself confronted on one side by a vast locker room that seemed to stretch to infinity and on the other by a room providing not only loos and basins, but showers, too.

She quickly crammed her coat and bag into an empty locker, stripped off her dress, tossed the shredded tights in a bin. There was no time for a shower so she dunked her feet, one at a time, in a basin of warm water to wash off the street dirt, half expecting Pam to burst in with the real elf at any minute.

She didn't but, until she did, she was grateful for being in the warm and, more importantly, in a very neat disguise.

She dabbed circles of rouge on her cheeks, scattered a few freckles across her nose, then a few more, before removing the nail polish that had been applied at great expense just hours ago. A shame, but clearly elves didn't have bright red nails.

Finally, she donned the costume, tucking her hair out of sight under the pointy felt hat and regarded herself in a handily placed mirror.

It wasn't a good look.

The green and white striped tights made her legs look fat and the tunic was doing her bum no favours. Right now, she didn't care.

Diary update: *The day has gone from bad to surreal. I've been mistaken for an elf. Not an entirely bad thing since I'm off the streets and I've been supplied, free of charge, with a neat disguise. It's just temporary, of course, like the new name. What I'm going to do when Hastings & Hart closes at eight o'clock is my next problem. But with luck I've got three hours*

*breathing space to work on a plan, always assuming
the real elf doesn't turn up in the meantime.*

*Three hours to get my breath back after
a very close encounter with Mr Tall, Dark and
Dangerous.*

Lucy ran her tongue over her lips to cool them, then shook
her head and stuffed her phone and her locker key into the
little leather pouch on her belt before presenting herself
for inspection.

Pam sighed, adjusted the hat so that a little more of her
hair showed. 'You've been a little heavy-handed with the
freckles.' Then, frowning, 'Is that a bruise?'

'It's nothing,' she said. 'Someone caught me with a bag,'
she said.

'The Underground just gets worse... Never mind.' She
took a small camera from her pocket. 'I'll just take a picture
for your ID. Say cheese...'

'Cheese.'

'Great. I'll log you into the system later. Sort you out a
swipe card.'

'Swipe card?'

'It's how we keep track of staff. How we know who is
working, how long they've worked and that they've left
the premises at the end of the day. You'll need it to get out
and, hopefully, get in again tomorrow.'

'Oh, right. Absolutely.'

'Come on. I'll take you to meet Frank Alyson, Deputy
Manager of the toy department and Chief Elf, and then you
can get started.'

She passed her over to a tall lugubrious man wearing
a long green tunic. She sort of sympathised with him. It
couldn't be much fun being a middle-aged man with his

dignity in shreds, but walking around Santa's grotto in a suit and tie would undoubtedly compromise the illusion.

'Louise Braithwaite,' Pam said, her voice fading to nothing as she introduced her. She cleared her throat, gathered herself. 'Be nice to this one. Elves don't grow on trees, you know.'

'Don't they? You surprise me. Most of them appear to have sawdust for brains.' He gave her a look that suggested he had no hopes that she had anything but wood pulp between the ears before turning back to Pam. 'You look ghastly. Go home. You'll be no use to anyone if you're ill.'

'And ho, ho, ho to you, too,' she said as she walked away.

'You could have handled that better,' Lucy said without thinking. She was good at that. Saying the first thing that came into her head. According to her file—the one she wasn't supposed to ever see—it had been her most usable asset. That and her passion. People would, apparently, *"… instantly warm to her enthusiasm, her natural openness and lack of guile…"*

They'd nailed that one.

It was saying the first thing that came into her head without thinking that had got her into this mess in the first place and now Frank was staring at her, clearly unused to criticism. Or maybe he was wondering where he'd seen her before.

'So, what happened to the last elf?' she said to distract him.

'She asked too many questions and I fed her to a troll,' he replied.

Sheesh…

'Anything else you'd like to know?'

She pressed her lips together and shook her head.

'Fast learner,' he replied with satisfaction. 'Keep it up and we'll get on.'

'Great.' She couldn't wait.

'So, Louise Braithwaite, what can you do?'

Do?

Wasn't standing about in a pointy hat and stripy tights enough?

Obviously not. Through a small window in his office, she could see an army of elves busily 'constructing' toys in Santa's workshop. They were dressing teddies and dolls, test-driving remote-controlled cars and encouraging children to join in and help them while they waited their turn to see Santa.

Otherwise known, if you happened to have a cynical turn of mind—and she'd just had a crash course in cynicism from a world master—as try-before-you-buy.

'Have you any experience?'

'Of being an elf?' Was he kidding? 'No,' she admitted quickly, 'but I am used to working with children. They tend to throw up when they get over-excited. Just tell me where the bucket and mop are kept and I'll cope.'

That earned her something that might have been a smile. 'Well, I have to admit that you're less of a fool than the last girl Pam brought me. She couldn't see past her mascara.'

Lucy resisted the urge to bat her expensively dyed eyelashes at him, but it was harder to keep the smile from breaking out. And why not? She was safe.

Without a pre-booked ticket, no one, not even Rupert's bodyguards, would be able to get beyond the entrance. More to the point, they'd realise that she couldn't either and wouldn't even bother. For the moment, at least, she could relax.

And what about grey eyes?

The thought popped, unbidden, into her head. The

thought of those eyes, a mouth that gave her goosebumps just thinking about it.

For heaven's sake, Lu…Louise Braithwaite, get a grip!

What would a man on his own be doing in Santa's grotto? And why would she care? He was the last person on earth she wanted to see.

Not that he'd recognize her dressed like this.

Even if, beneath the rouge and abundant freckles, someone spotted a passing resemblance to the face that had been on the front cover of *Celebrity* magazine a dozen or more times in the last few months, they would dismiss it. Why, after all, would Lucy B, aka Cinderella, be working as an elf in a department store?

'You can start by tidying up, straightening shelves while you find your way around. When you've done that you can take the empty space on the bench, dressing dolls and teddies. You'll have to fit in a break with the rest of the staff.'

'Right. Thanks.'

She stood in the doorway for a moment, taking a look around, familiarising herself with the layout before launching herself into the mix of elves, children and parents.

This was all new to her. Shunted around the care system all her life, she'd never been taken to see 'Santa' when she was a child. Even if she had got lucky, it would never have been like this.

The grotto had been designed to give children the illusion that they were in Santa's North Pole workshop and there was a touch of magic about it that only a high-end designer—and a great deal of money—could have achieved. She didn't know about the kids, but it certainly worked for her.

She was still taking it all in when there was a tug on the

hem of her tunic and she turned to find herself looking at the child from the lift.

'You're not an elf,' she declared loudly. 'I saw you out there—' she pointed dramatically '—in the real world.'

Oh... fairy lights!

Having done her best to restore a little girl's faith in Santa, she'd immediately shattered it.

Maybe that was the message. There are no such things as fairy tales. On the other hand, if she'd had a moment or two of fantasy as a child, she might not have grabbed so desperately for it as an adult.

But this was not about her and, putting her finger to her lips in a quick, 'Shh!' she folded herself up so that she was on the same level as the child. 'What's your name?'

'Dido.'

'Can you keep a secret, Dido?'

The child, thumb stuck firmly back in her mouth, nodded once.

'Well, that's great because this is a really huge secret,' she said. 'You're absolutely right. You did see me in the lift, but the reason I was up there in the real world was because I was on a special mission from Santa.'

She hadn't worked as an assistant in a day-care nursery for years without learning how to spin a story. The pity of it was that she hadn't learned to spot one when it was being spun at her.

'What's a mishun?'

'A very special task. The toughest. I shouldn't be telling you this, but the thing is that Rudolph—'

'Rudolph?' Eyes wide, Dido abandoned the comfort of the thumb.

'Rudolph,' she repeated, 'had run out of his favourite snack. I had to disguise myself as a human, go up to the food hall—'

'Is he here?'

Lucy raised her finger to her lips again and then pointed it towards the ceiling. 'He's up there, on the roof with all the other reindeer,' she whispered. 'As soon as the store closes on Christmas Eve, we're going to load up the sleigh and off they'll go.'

'Really?' she whispered back, eyes like saucers.

'Elf's honour,' she said, crossing her heart.

'Can I see him?'

Oh, good grief... 'He's resting, Dido. Building up his strength. It's a big job delivering presents to all the children in the world.'

'I 'spose...' For a moment her little face sagged with disappointment, then she said, 'Was it a carrot? His favourite snack? We always leave a carrot for Rudolph.'

'Well, carrots are good, obviously,' she said, wondering what the rest of the poor reindeer had to sustain them. 'Great for his eyesight as he flies through the night. Good for children, too.' Good for you was so boring, though. Christmas was about excitement, magic. 'But what Rudolph really loves when it's cold is a handful of chilli-flavoured cashew nuts to warm him up.' She paused. 'They're what make his nose glow.'

'Wow! Really? That is so cool...'

'That's a very special secret,' Lucy warned. 'Between you, me, Rudolph and Santa.'

'So I can't tell Cleo? She's my big sister.'

'The sister who tried to tell you that Santa doesn't exist? I doooon't think so.'

The child giggled.

'Only a very small handful, though. If Rudolph has too many his nose will overheat...'

Stop! Stop it right there, Lucy Bright!

'Dido... It's time to go,' her mother said, rescuing her.

Mouthing a silent *thank you* over her daughter's head. 'Say bye-bye.'

'Bye-bye.' Then she whispered, 'Say hi to Rudolph.'

'I will.' Lucy put her finger to her lip, then said, 'Merry Christmas.'

'Merry Christmas.'

Whew. The magic restored to one little innocent. Clap if you believe in fairies…

Not her.

Not fairies. Not fairy tales.

Lesson learned.

She looked up, saw the Chief Elf watching her from his little window and, as ordered, began picking up toys that had been picked up and dropped, restoring them to the shelves. Holding the hands of children who'd momentarily lost sight of their mothers.

When all was calm and ordered, she hitched herself onto the vacant stool and began buttoning teddies into jackets and trousers. While her fingers moved on automatic, she found herself wondering not about her future, or where she was going to spend the night, but about the man on the stairs. The way he'd caught her, held her for what seemed like minutes rather than seconds.

The broad support on his hand at her back. Dangerously mesmerising grey eyes that had locked into hers, turning her on, lighting her up like the national grid. She could still feel the fizz of it. She'd never understood why men talked about taking a 'cold shower' until now.

'Any trouble evicting the bodyguards?' Nat asked, dropping in at the security office in the basement. It was hopeless hunting through the store, but he might catch a glimpse of her on the bank of screens being fed images from CCTV cameras around the store.

'No, although they were on the phone calling up reinforcements before they were through the door. Whoever replaces them won't be as easy to spot.'

Women. He'd use women, he thought, scanning the screens but she'd gone to earth. Found a hiding place. Or perhaps she really had slipped back out into the dark streets. That should have been his hope; instead, the idea of her out there, alone in the cold and dark, filled him with dread.

'Have you seen them before?' he pressed. 'Any idea who they work for?'

Bryan Matthews, his security chief, frowned, clearly puzzled by his interest, but shook his head, keeping whatever he was thinking to himself.

'They didn't say anything? Offer any explanation?'

'No, they were clam-mouthed professionals. They must have been in a flat panic to have drawn attention to themselves like that. Any idea who they've lost?'

'Maybe. It's possible that she's about this high,' he said, his hand level with his chin. 'Short pale blonde hair, green eyes, wearing a black knitted dress with a big collar.' He looked at the shoe he was still carrying. 'And no shoes.'

'You saw her?'

He'd done more than that. He'd not just seen her, but caught her, held her and she'd filled up his senses like a well after a drought. There had been a connection between them so physical that when she'd run it had felt as if she'd torn away a chunk of his flesh and taken it with her.

'I saw someone who seemed to be in a bit of a state,' he said. 'Pass the word to keep alert for anything out of the ordinary, especially at the store exits. When she does leave I want to be sure it's her decision. Any problem, call me.'

'I'll pass the word.'

He nodded. 'I'll be in my office.'

He glanced once more at the screens, not knowing whether to be relieved or disappointed when he came up empty.

The common sense response would be relief, he reminded himself as he strode through the electrical department, heading for the lift. But this was about more than the smooth running of the store. It was rare for a woman to catch his attention with such immediacy.

Her fear had only sharpened his reaction, taking it beyond simple interest in an attractive woman. A snatched moment that had raised his heart rate, leaving him not just breathless, but exposed, naked, defenceless. The kind of feelings he hated, did everything possible to avoid. But still he wanted to know who she was. What, who, she was running from. Wanted to taste lips that had been close enough to tantalise his memory, send heat spiralling down through his body…

He came to an abrupt halt as he realised that she was there. Right there in front of him. Not just once, but over and over, her face looking out from dozens of silent television screens banked up against the wall. Her hair was longer, her face fuller and she was smiling so that those green eyes sparkled. The heat intensified as he focused on her lips. How close had he come to kissing her?

Close enough to imagine how it would feel, the softness of her lips, how she tasted as her body softened beneath him…

Whoever she was, it seemed that her disappearance was important enough to make the national news.

Or maybe just dramatic enough.

He reached the nearest set and as he brought up the sound the picture switched to a ruckus at a press conference.

'…*scenes of total confusion as she very publicly ended*

her engagement to financier, Rupert Henshawe, accusing him of being a liar and a cheat...'

The camera caught Henshawe's startled face, moving in for a close-up of a trickle of blood that appeared on his cheek, before swinging wildly to catch the green-eyed girl clutching a file against her breast with one hand, while swinging her bag, connecting with the jaw of a man who was trying to hang on to her with the other.

The picture faded to the familiar figure of business tycoon, Rupert Henshawe, making a statement to camera.

'I blame myself. I should have realised that such a change in lifestyle would lead to stress in someone unused to the difficulty of being always in the public eye—'

His phone rang. He ignored it.

'Meeting Lucy was a life-changing moment for me. She's encouraged me to see the world in a new light...'

Lucy. Her name was Lucy.

'...her passionate belief in the fair trade movement has given a new ethical dimension to our fashion chain, which today I'm relaunching under the new name, Lucy B, in her honour...'

That was why she'd looked familiar, he realised as Henshawe paused, apparently struggling to keep back the tears.

He'd seen something in the papers about a romance with some girl who worked in his office—about as likely as Henshawe becoming a planet-hugger, he'd have thought...

'Yes?' he snapped, finally responding to the phone's insistent ring, never taking his eyes from the screen.

'It's Pam Wootton, Nat—'

'...I realise that I have been too wrapped up in all these new initiatives, visiting overseas suppliers, to give her the

support she so desperately needed. To notice how tired she has become, her lack of appetite, her growing dependence on the tranquillisers that were prescribed after the press drove her to move out of the flat she shared with friends—'

Tranquillisers?

Nat felt a cold chill run through him. History repeating itself...

'She needs rest, time to recover, all my best care and, as soon as I have found her, I will ensure—'

'Nat?'

The voice in his ear was so insistent that he realised it wasn't the first time his PA had said his name.

'Sorry, Meg, I was distracted,' he said, still staring at the screen. Then, as the news moved on to another story and he forced himself to concentrate, 'Pam Wootton? What's the matter with her?'

'She's collapsed. She was down in the grotto when it happened and Frank Alyson has called an ambulance, but I thought you'd want to know.'

'I'll be right there.'

'What are you doing?'

Lucy, teddy-dressing on automatic while her brain frantically free-wheeled—desperately trying to forget the man with the grey eyes and concentrate on thinking about where she could go when the store closed—looked up to find a small boy watching her.

'I'm wrapping this teddy up in a warm coat. It's snowing,' she said, glad of a distraction. Short of a park bench, she was out of ideas. 'It will be very cold on Santa's sleigh.'

'Can I help?'

'James, don't be a nuisance,' his mother warned. She

had two smaller girls clutching at her skirts, half scared, half bewitched. Lucy smiled reassuringly.

'He's fine,' she said. 'Do you all want to give me a hand?'

Within minutes she was surrounded by small children dressing teddies, grinning happily as she helped with sleeves and buttons.

How long had it been since she'd done that? Not a posed for the camera smile, the kind that made your face ache, but an honest-to-goodness grin?

She'd been so busy shopping, being interviewed by the gossip magazines, having her photograph taken, that there hadn't been any time to catch her breath, let alone enjoy the crazy roller coaster ride she was on. Or maybe that was the point.

She hadn't wanted time to stop and think because if she had, she would have had to listen to the still small voice whispering away in the back of her mind telling her that it couldn't possibly be real.

Mental note for diary: always listen to still small voice. It knows what it's talking about.

Being here reminded her of how much she'd missed working in the day-care nursery. Missed the children.

'Your turn for a break,' one of the elves said, as it was time for the children to get back on the sleigh, and she began to gather up the bears. 'Through the office, turn left. Coffee, tea, biscuits are on the house. There's a machine with snacks if you need anything else.'

The tea was welcome and although Lucy wasn't hungry she took a biscuit. Who knew when she'd get the chance to eat again? With that thought in mind, she stocked up on chocolate and crisps from the machine.

Rather than get involved in conversation with the other staff, she took a moment to check her phone, although what she was expecting to find, she didn't know. Or rather she did. Dozens of missed calls, all of which she ignored. Texts, too. And hundreds of tweets, all demanding to know the whereabouts of Cinderella.

They couldn't all have been from Rupert's stooges. But how could she tell the real from the phoney? If someone was hoping to entice her into trusting them, they wouldn't be leaping to his defence, would they?

She was considering whether to send a tweet to reassure the good guys that she was safe—at least for now—when something made her look up. The same prickle of awareness that had made her look around on the stairs.

And for the same reason.

There, not ten feet away, talking to Frank Alyson, was the man with grey eyes. The man who'd caught her, held her in one hand as easily as if she were a child and who had, for one brief moment, made her forget everything. Where she was, why she was running…

She could still feel the imprint of his hand on her back, the warmth of his breath against her cheek and, as she sucked her lower lip into her mouth to cool it, she almost believed that she could taste him on her tongue.

CHAPTER FOUR

GREY Eyes was head to head with the Chief Elf and Lucy scarcely dared breathe as she watched the pair of them.

One look and the game would be up.

It was one thing keeping her identity a secret from people who weren't looking for her, didn't expect to see her, but anyone who knew her, or was looking for her, wouldn't be fooled for a moment by her disguise. And he had to be looking for her. Didn't he?

The thought filled her with a mixture of dread and elation. While her head was afraid, she had to restrain her body from leaning towards him, from shouting *Look! Here I am!*

But, standing back like this so that she could see all of him—the broad shoulders, the long legs—she could also see that he was wearing an identity tag just like the one Pam had been wearing, which meant that he wasn't a customer, someone just passing through.

He worked in the store and if Rupert's bodyguards had elicited help from the management in finding her she was in deep trouble because one thing was obvious. He wasn't junior staff.

His pinstriped suit was the business, his tie, navy with a tiny pattern, was eye-wateringly expensive; she'd bought one like it in the store just yesterday. And, even without the designer gear, he had that unmistakable air of authority.

But if she'd thought he'd seemed intense as he'd held her balanced above the stairs, now he looked positively grim.

'Keep your eyes open, Frank.' His voice was low; he didn't need to raise it to make a point.

As she watched, pinned to the spot, he took a step back, glanced around, his eyes momentarily coming to rest on her. She'd left it too late to move and she lowered her lashes, opting for the if-I-can't-see-you-then-you-can't-see-me scenario. Holding her breath as she waited for the *got you* hand on the shoulder.

Her heart ceased to beat for the second or two that he continued to stare at her, but after a moment she realised that, while he was looking at her, he wasn't actually seeing her. He wasn't even in this room, not in his head, anyway.

Then someone put his head around the corner. 'Whenever you're ready, sir.'

Without a word, he turned and walked away. Which was when she realised that he was gripping something in his hand. A shoe.

Her shoe.

Had it fallen out of her bag when she'd stumbled?

Well, duh... How many red suede peep-toe designer shoes were there lying around Hastings & Hart? How many dumb females whose coach had just turned into a pumpkin were there fleeing up the H&H stairs scattering footwear in their wake?

How many men who could stop your heart with a look?

Stop it!

Enough with the fairy tales.

She was done with fairy tales.

'Wh…who was that?' she asked, as casually as she could, once she'd finally managed to retrieve her heart from her mouth and coax it back into life.

Frank gave her a weary look and she remembered, too late, that he didn't like inquisitive elves.

'That, Miss Mop and Bucket,' he replied, 'was Nathaniel Hart.'

'Hart?' She blinked. 'As in…' She pointed up at the building soaring above them.

'As in Hastings & Hart,' he confirmed.

'No…' Or, to put it another way, *Nooooooo!*

'Are you arguing with me?'

'No!' And she shook her head, to make sure. 'I just hadn't realised there was a real Mr Hart.' It certainly explained the air of authority. If he looked as if he owned the place it was because, well, he did. 'I thought that most of these big stores were owned by big chains.'

'Hastings & Hart is not most stores.'

About to ask if there was a Mr Hastings, or even a Mrs Hart, she thought better of it. She was having a bad enough day without feeling guilty about lusting after some woman's husband.

'Is that all?' Frank asked with a sardonic lift of the brow. 'Or are you prepared to honour us with another teddy-dressing class for the under fives?'

'I'm sorry. It got a bit out of hand,' she said, fairly sure that was sarcasm rather than praise. 'I won't do it again.'

'Oh, please don't let me stop you. You are a hit with the children, if not with their mothers.'

Definitely sarcasm and she had been feeling rather guilty since several of the children had refused point-blank to surrender their bears to the rigours of a freezing sleigh ride and insisted they come home with them in a nice warm taxi. Not that it should worry Frank Alyson. It was all the more profit for Nathaniel Hart, wasn't it? Which was all men like him cared about.

But all the practice she'd had smiling in the last few months stood her in good stead and she gave him one of her best.

He looked somewhat startled, as well he might—she didn't imagine he got too many of those—and, satisfied with the effect, she returned to her stool, where she would be safely out of sight of Mr Nathaniel Hart, unless he borrowed Frank Alyson's Chief Elf robes.

But, while the children kept her busy, her brain was fizzing with questions. Had Grey Eyes been contacted directly by one of Rupert's minions? Asked to organise a discreet search for her? Or even perhaps by Rupert himself? They probably knew one another—billionaires united was a very small club—because he seemed to be taking a personal interest in the search.

He hadn't sounded at all happy when, having belatedly come to her senses, she'd taken off up the stairs, leaving only her shoe behind.

And it would explain why he was carrying it around with him. He assumed that she had the other one tucked away in her bag and, obviously, she would need two of them if she was going to walk out of here.

Tough. He should have kept his mind on the job.

Or maybe not. Even now, her heart flipped at the memory as she absently sucked on an overheated lip.

Having been assured by the paramedics that Pam was suffering from nothing worse than the latest bug that was going around, Nat drove her home and insisted that she stay there until she was fully recovered.

'But how will you cope? There's so much to do and—'

'Pam, we'll manage,' he insisted. 'And the last thing we need at this time of year is an epidemic.'

'Sorry. I know. And no one's indispensable. Petra will manage. Probably.' She rubbed at her temple. 'There was something I was meant to be doing...' He waited, but she sighed and said, 'No, it's gone.'

'Can I get you anything? Tea? Juice?'

'You're a sweet man, Nathaniel Hart,' she croaked. 'You'd make some woman a lovely husband.'

An image of the woman on the stairs, her scent, the softness of her dress, disturbingly real, filled his head...

'I'm just a details man,' he said, blanking it off. 'Go and get into bed. I'll make you a hot drink.'

'You should get back to London before the roads get any worse,' she said. Then, as headlights swept across the window, 'That's Peter home.'

'Closing time, Lou.' The elf sitting on the next stool stood up, eased her back. 'Reality beckons.'

'I'll just finish dressing this bear.'

'You're keen. See you tomorrow.'

It was a casual throwaway line, needing no answer, and Lucy didn't reply. Tomorrow would have to take care of itself; it was tonight that was the problem.

She tucked the teddy into a pair of striped pyjamas and a dressing gown, putting off the moment when she'd have to face a cold world. Because no amount of thinking had provided her with an answer to where she could go. Certainly not the flat she'd shared before she'd met Rupert. That would be the first place anyone would look.

She had a little money in her purse that would cover a night at some cheap B&B. The problem with that was that her face would be all over the evening news and someone was bound to spot her and call it in to one of the tabloids for the tip-off money.

The sensible answer, she knew, would be to contact one of them herself, let them take care of her. They'd stick her in a safe house so that no one else could get to her and they'd pay well for the story she had to tell. That was the reason they'd been grabbing at her, chasing after her. Why Rupert would be equally anxious to keep her away from them.

The problem with going down that route was that there would be no way back to her real life.

Once she'd taken their money she'd be their property. Would never be able to go back to being the person she had been six months ago.

Instead she'd become one of those pathetic Z-list celebrities who were forever doomed to live off their moment of infamy, relying on ever more sleazy stories to keep themselves in the public eye. Because no one would employ her in a nursery or day-care centre ever again.

But this reprieve was temporary. Out of time, she placed the teddy on the shelf and went to the office.

Frank looked up from his desk, where he was inputting figures into a computer. 'Are you still here?'

'Apparently. I was looking for Pam.'

He pulled a face. 'She collapsed not long after you arrived,' he said in an I-told-you-so tone of voice.

'Oh, good grief. I'm so sorry. Is she going to be all right?'

'It's just a bug and an inability to accept that we can manage without her for a day or two. Mr Hart took her home a couple of hours ago. Why did you want her?'

'Well...'

About to explain about the swipe card, it occurred to her that if Pam had collapsed not long after she'd mistaken her for an elf, she might not have had time to do the paperwork. Make her official. Log her in.

'It's nothing that won't wait. Although…'

She couldn't. Could she?

'She didn't mention what time I'm supposed to start tomorrow,' she added, as casually as she could.

'The store opens at ten. If you're honouring us with your presence, you'll need to be in your place, teddy at the ready at one minute to. Is that it?'

'Er…yes. Ten. No problem.'

He nodded. 'Goodnight.' Then, as she reached the door, 'You did a good job, Louise. I hope we'll see you tomorrow.'

'Thanks,' she said. 'Me, too.'

Nat switched on the radio as he drove back through thick swirling snowflakes that were beginning to pile up on the edges of the road. The footpaths were already white.

He'd hoped to catch an update about Henshawe's missing fiancée—ex-fiancée—on the news, but it was all weather warnings and travel news and the bulletins focused on the mounting chaos as commuters tried to get home in weather that hadn't been forecast.

She'd got lucky. But not as lucky as Henshawe. An embarrassing story was going to be buried under tomorrow's headlines about drivers spending the night in their cars, complaints about incompetent weather forecasters and the lack of grit on the roads.

They'd probably be reunited and back on the front cover of some gossip magazine by next week, with whatever indiscretions she was accusing him of long forgotten, he told himself. Forget her.

By the time he returned to the store it was closing. The last few shoppers were being ushered through the doors, the cloakrooms and changing rooms thoroughly checked in a well rehearsed routine to flush out anyone who might harbour ideas of spending the night there.

He parked in the underground garage, removed the shoe from the glove compartment and walked through to the security office.

Bryan looked up as he entered.

'Anything?' he asked.

'Not a sign. She probably slipped out under cover of the crowds. She's certainly not in the store now.'

'No.' He looked at the shoe and, instead of dropping it in the lost property box, held onto it.

'Are you going straight up to the tenth floor?'

He nodded. 'I'll be in the office for a while. You're working late?'

'We're a couple of men down with some bug that's going around.'

'Let me know if it becomes a problem.'

But it wasn't the likelihood of staff shortages at their busiest time of year that was nagging at him as he headed for the lifts. It was something he'd seen, something telling him that, despite all evidence to the contrary, his fugitive hadn't gone anywhere. That she was still here.

It was stupid, he knew.

She'd undoubtedly used the phone she'd been clutching in the hand she'd flung around his neck to call a friend, someone to bring her a change of clothes and whatever else she needed.

He needed to put the incident out of his mind. Forget the impact of her eyes, the flawless skin, long lashes that had been burned into his brain like a photograph in that long moment when he'd held her.

What was it? What was he missing?

He walked through the electrical department, but the

television screens that had been filled with her larger-than-life-size image were all blank now.

Her hair had been darker in that photograph. She'd been wearing less make-up. It was almost like seeing a before and after photograph. The original and the made-over version. Thinner, the image expensively finished, refined, everything except a tiny beauty spot above her lip that could not be airbrushed out of reality...

He stopped.

The beauty spot. That was what he'd seen. He scanned his memory, fast-forwarding through everything he'd seen and done in the hours since that moment on the stairs.

And came skidding to a halt on the elf.

The one who'd been standing so still by the drinks machine while he was talking to Frank. She was the right height, the right shape—filling out the elf costume in a way it hadn't been designed for. And she'd had a beauty spot in exactly the same place as the girl on the stairs.

Coincidence? Maybe, but he spun around and headed into the grotto.

While everyone else raced to change, get away as quickly as possible, Lucy dawdled and it had taken remarkably little time for the locker room to empty.

It was a little eerie being there on her own, the motion-sensitive lights shutting down all around her, leaving her in just a small area of light. And, while she was grateful to be off the streets, in the warm, she wasn't entirely sure what to do next.

Where she would be safe.

While the locker rooms would be free of cameras—she was almost certain they would be free of cameras—there would undoubtedly be a security presence of some sort.

Would it be high-tech gadgetry? Motion sensors, that

sort of thing. Patrols? Or just someone tucked up in an office with a flask of coffee, a pile of sandwiches and a good book while he monitored the store cameras?

At least she would be safe in here for a little while and she could use the time to take the shower she'd longed for. Wash off the whole hideous day. Wash off the last few months and reclaim herself.

And if someone did happen to come in, check that everyone had left, she could surely come up with some believable reason for staying behind to take a shower after work.

A hot date?

Actually, she did have one of those. Well, a date, anyway. Rupert didn't do hot, but neither would he cancel the Lucy B launch dinner at The Ritz just because she'd caused him a little embarrassment. She had no doubt that his PR team had already put some kind of spin on that. Stress. Pre-wedding nerves.

Of course if she turned up in the elf costume—the paparazzi would certainly be on the job tonight—it would wipe the smug smile off all their faces.

For a moment she was sorely tempted but, recalling the scrum at the press conference, she decided to give it a miss.

No. If she needed an excuse for being in the shower so late, she'd stick to the second job story. Everyone needed extra money at Christmas and a waitress—her own particular preference when she'd needed the cash to finance her studies—had to be clean and fresh.

She reclaimed her dress from the locker and then, having folded her costume neatly and left it on the bench, she took a towel from the rack and stepped into one of the stalls.

The water was hot and there were shampoo and soap dispensers. Hastings & Hart staff were very well taken care of, she decided, as she pushed the pump for a dollop of soap. Maybe she should reconsider her career options.

Could being an elf in a department store be considered a career? What did Santa do for the rest of the year? And would she get to meet the boss again?

Cold shower, cold shower!

She squeezed some shampoo. Her hair didn't need washing—she'd spent two hours in the salon having it cut and pampered earlier in the day—but she felt the need to cleanse herself from top to toe, rid herself of the past few months, and she dug in deep with her fingers, washing away the scent of betrayal, rinsing it down the drain.

Then, in no hurry to stop, she reached out to adjust the temperature a touch.

The grotto, Santa's workshop, was deserted. Nat walked through to Frank's office, hoping he might find a staff list, but the man was too well organised to leave such things lying about. Besides, he knew he had to be wrong. It had to be a coincidence. There was no way Lucy could have transformed herself into an elf.

It was ridiculous. He was becoming obsessed, seeing things.

Hearing things…

A deluge of ice water hit Lucy and she let out a shriek that would have woken the dead. She groped blindly for the control which, having spun at the merest touch, was now stuck stubbornly on cold.

She gave one last tug. The control knob came off in her hand and, freezing, she burst out of the shower stall, dripping, naked, eyes closed as she grabbed for the towel.

She wiped her face, took a breath, opened her eyes and discovered that she was not alone.

Nathaniel Hart—the man with his name above the front door—had obviously heard her yell. More of her 'openness and lack of guile', obviously. Not her best move if she wanted to keep below the radar.

She didn't scream, despite the shock. Her mouth opened; her brain was sending all the right signals but nothing was getting past the big thick lump that was blocking her throat.

He took the control from her hand, reached into the shower stall, screwed it deftly back into place and turned off the water, giving her a chance to gather her wits and wrap the towel around her before he closed the door.

Then he helped himself to one, dried his hands and only when he'd tossed it onto the bench behind her did he give her his full attention.

'Making yourself at home, Cinderella?' he enquired after what felt like the longest moment in her life while a slow blush spread from her cheeks and down her neck, heating all points south until it reached her toes.

Cinderella.

He knew...

It took forever to unglue her tongue from the roof of her mouth, making her lips work.

She took a step back, slipped on a floor awash with cold water. Torn between grabbing for safety and hanging onto the towel, she made a grab for the shower door.

No doubt afraid that she'd bring that down on them, Nathaniel Hart reached for her arm, steadying her before the towel had slipped more than an inch.

An inch was way too much. The towel, which when she'd first picked it up had seemed perfectly adequate for decency, now felt like a pocket handkerchief.

'This is the women's locker room,' she finally managed.

As if that was going to make any difference. This was

his store and she was trapped. Not just shoeless this time, but 'less' just about everything except for a teeny, tiny towel that just about covered her from breast to thigh. Not nearly enough when this close to a man who'd sizzled her with a look when she'd been fully dressed.

He was looking now—which dealt with freezing...

'You shouldn't be here,' she said, finally managing to get her voice to work and going for indignant. She failed miserably. She just sounded breathless. She felt breathless...

With good reason.

She was naked, alone and at the mercy of a man who almost certainly meant her no good. But, far from fleeing, his touch was like an electric charge and all her instincts were telling her to forget modesty, let the towel fall and cooperate with whatever he had in mind. One hundred per cent.

Nooooo!

She forced herself to take a step away, put some distance between them, get a grip. Regretting it the minute she did. There was something about his touch that made her feel safe. Made her feel...

'And that's not my name,' she added, cutting off the thought before she lost it entirely.

'No?' He flipped something from his pocket and offered it to her. 'If the shoe fits...'

He was still carrying her shoe?

'What do you think this is?' she demanded, ignoring the shoe. 'A pantomime? I'm all through with the Cinderella thing, Mr Hart.'

'You know who I am?'

'Mr Alyson told me. You're Nathaniel Hart and you own this store.'

'I run it. Not the same thing.'

'Oh.' She wasn't sure why that was better, but somehow

it was. She was totally off billionaire tycoons. 'I just assumed...'

'Most people do.'

'Well, if the name fits,' she said and thought she got the tiniest response. Just a hint of a smile. But maybe she was imagining it. 'What do you want, Mr Hart?'

'Nothing. On the contrary, I'm your fairy godmother.'

She stared at him but said nothing. She was in enough trouble without stating the obvious.

'I know what you're thinking,' he said.

'I promise you, you haven't got a clue.'

'You're thinking where is the frilly skirt? Where are the wings?'

No... Not even close. 'Trust me, it would not be a good look for you. Take my advice, stick with the pin-stripes.'

'Well, I'm glad you take that view.'

The barest suspicion of a smile became a twitch of the lips, curling around her, warm, enticing. Tempting. Heating up bits that it would take a very long cold shower to beat into line and she was very glad indeed that he hadn't got a clue.

'Hastings & Hart takes its role as an equal opportunities employer very seriously,' he assured her.

'We have to take our fairy godmothers wherever we can find them in these enlightened days,' she agreed, firmly resisting the temptation to fling herself into his arms and invite him to make free with his magic wand. Instead, she tightened her lips, keeping them pressed down in a straight line. A smile meant nothing, she told herself. Anyone could smile. It was easy. You just stretched your lips wide...

But he was really good at it. It wasn't just the corner of his mouth doing something that hit all the right buttons. It had reached all the way up to his eyes and the warmth of it reached deep within her, turning her insides liquid.

She clutched the towel a little tighter. 'I guess the real test comes with Santa Claus? Would you employ a woman for that role?' she asked a touch desperately.

The lines carved into his cheeks became deeper, bracketing his mouth. And the silver sparks in his eyes had not been reflections of the Christmas decorations, she realised, but were all his own. It was all there now. Every part of his face was engaged and while it wasn't a pretty smile, it was all the more dangerous for that.

'Not my decision, thank goodness. Human Resources have the responsibility of employing the best person for the job and keeping me on the right side of the law.'

She tutted. 'Passing the buck.'

'There has to be some advantage to go with the name,' he replied, 'but, as far as fairy godmothers go, right now I'm not just your best option, I appear to be the only one.'

'Oh?' she said, putting on a brave front. If she was going down, she refused to be a pushover. 'Why do you think that?'

'Because if there had been anyone you could ask for help you wouldn't be hiding out in Santa's grotto dressed as an elf. You'd have used the phone you were carrying to call them.'

'Who says I'm hiding?' she demanded. 'That I need help.'

'The fact that you're here, prepared to risk getting caught on the premises after closing, speaks for itself.'

She couldn't argue with his logic. He had it, spot on, but she still had the backup excuse. 'I'm just late leaving,' she said. 'I needed a shower before I start my other job.'

He shook his head.

'You're not buying it?'

'Sorry.'

'Oh, well. It was worth a shot.' She managed a shrug

even though her heart was hammering in her mouth. 'So. What happens now?'

'I congratulate you on your ingenuity?' he suggested. 'Ask how you managed to get yourself kitted out with an elf costume so that you could hide out in Santa's grotto?'

'I'm smart?'

'Obviously. But, if you managed it, there are security issues involved.'

'Oh, look, it wasn't anyone's fault,' she said quickly. Clearly the game was up for her, but she couldn't allow anyone else to suffer. 'I was mistaken for a temp who was expected but never turned up and it was too good an opportunity to miss. Pam won't get into trouble, will she? She was desperate. Not just desperate but sick,' she stressed. 'Well, you know that since you took her home.'

'Don't worry about Pam, worry about yourself,' he said, the smile fading.

She shivered. Not from fear. This man was not a bully. He wasn't crowding her, there was no suggestion of the physical threat that had seemed so real in the press conference. Why she'd run.

He was much more dangerous than that.

He could bring her down with a look. As if to prove it, he reached for a dry towel and draped it around her shoulders, assuming that she was cold. His touch tingled through her and she knew that all he had to do was put his hand to her back and she'd put up her hands, surrender without a struggle.

Fortunately, he didn't know that.

'What were you planning to do next?' he asked, not lingering, but taking a step back, putting clear air between them.

'Get dressed?' she suggested.

'And then?' he persisted.

'I thought I might bed down in one of your tents.' There seemed little point in lying about it. 'I noticed them yesterday when I was Christmas shopping. I've never been camping,' she added.

'It's overrated. Especially in the middle of winter.'

'I don't know. I could brew myself some tea on one of those little camp stoves. Fry a few sausages for my supper. I'd leave the money for the food on the till in the food hall.' She clutched the towel a little more tightly against her bosom. 'Maybe have a bit of a sing-song to keep my spirits up,' she added a touch recklessly. 'I did work for three hours for nothing. And I was planning to work tomorrow on the same terms. Bed and breakfast seems a reasonable exchange.'

'More than reasonable,' he agreed. 'Which one did you have your eye on?'

'I'm sorry?'

'Which tent? I can recommend the one-man Himalayan. I'm told that it's absolutely draught-proof.'

'Oh. Right. Well, thanks.'

'I'd strongly advise against the cooking, though. The security staff are based on the same floor and the smoke alarms are extremely sensitive.'

CHAPTER FIVE

Lucy swallowed hard. Was he joking? It was impossible to tell. When he wasn't smiling, Nathaniel Hart could give lessons in how to do a poker face.

'Well, thanks for the tip,' she managed. 'I've got a bag of crisps and a chocolate biscuit that I bought from the machine. They'll keep me going.'

He shook his head and a lick of thick dark hair slid across his forehead.

'That won't do,' he said, combing it back with long fingers. 'Chocolate biscuits and crisps aren't going to provide you with your five-a-day.'

Her five-a-day? She stared him. Unreal. The man was not only conspiring with her to trespass in his department store, but he was concerned that she was eating healthily. Consuming the government's daily recommended five portions of fruit and vegetables...

Or had he already summoned Rupert and was simply amusing himself at her expense while he waited for him to arrive and remove her?

Of course he was. Why was she even wasting time thinking about it?

'Who are you? The food police?' she demanded crossly. At least that was the intent but his hand was still on her arm, his fingers warm against her goosepimply skin and she didn't sound cross. She sounded breathless.

'Hastings & Hart take a close interest in staff welfare. We have a cycle to work scheme—which is why you have the luxury of shower facilities—'

'Luxury!' Finally she got her voice back. But then there wasn't much luxury in an unexpected ice-cold dunk.

'—and subsidised gym membership as well as a healthy options menu in the staff canteen.'

And he'd driven Pam Wootton home when she was taken ill, she reminded herself. That was taking staff welfare very seriously indeed. Not many men in his position would have done that. It suggested that he was unusually kind, thoughtful and, about to tell herself that Rupert would never have done that, it occurred to her that he had. Done exactly that. And, as she'd just discovered, he was neither kind nor thoughtful.

'Impressive, Mr Hart, but I'm only a temp. Temps don't get fringe benefits.'

Not just a temp, but an illicit one at that. He might be a great employer but she had no more reason to trust him than he had to trust her.

'Besides, the crisps are made from potatoes,' she said, playing for time as she tried, desperately, to think what to do next. Pull away from his hand, for a start, obviously. Put some space between them…'And they're cheese and onion flavour.'

There were no windows down here, but even in the basement there had to be a fire escape. Or would Rupert have learned from her last dash for freedom and have those covered before he moved in?

Was that what all the time-wasting was about?

'So potato and onion, that's two of my five,' she added, wishing she'd spent more time thinking about her escape instead of day-dreaming about a dishy stranger while she dressed teddy bears. 'There's the protein from the cheese, too, don't forget.'

Think... *Think!*

'And it's an orange chocolate biscuit.'

'Is that it?' he asked. 'All done?'

'All done,' she admitted. She was out of ideas. Out of excuses. Out of flavourings.

'Nice try—'

There was the smile again. The whole works. Crinkles fanning out from the corners of his eyes, something magical happening to his mouth as the lower lip softened to reveal the merest glimpse of white teeth. And then there were his eyes...

His eyes seemed to suggest that he was as surprised as she was to find he was smiling and, as quickly as it had appeared, it vanished.

And she could breathe again.

'—but no cigar,' he said. 'I'm sorry to be the bearer of bad news but potatoes don't count as a vegetable.'

'They don't?' She made a good fist at surprised.

'Not as one of your five-a-day.'

He didn't look sorry.

'You're telling me I'm going to have to stop counting fries?' she demanded, hoping to make him forget himself again and actually laugh. Get him on her side. 'Well, that's a swizz.'

'And you can forget the flavourings, too.'

'I was afraid that might be stretching it. I did have orange juice with my breakfast,' she assured him, as if determined to prove that she wasn't a complete dietary failure. Playing the fool in an attempt to lull him into believing that she'd bought his act.

'Good start. And since breakfast?'

'I had green beans with my lunch and I'm fairly sure that the fruit in the dessert was the real thing.'

'Apple tart, right?'

'How on earth do you know that?'

'The cinnamon was the giveaway.'

'Cinnamon?' Had he been that close? Mortified, she smothered a groan. Time to put a stop to this. 'What about you, Mr Hart?'

'Nat.'

'Nat?'

'Short for Nathaniel. A bit of a mouthful.'

'But nicer than Nat, which is a small spiteful insect which takes lumps out of you when you're innocently enjoying a sunset.'

'Very nearly,' he agreed, rewarding her with a flicker of a smile that went straight to her blush. And too late she realised her mistake. 'What about me?'

She'd thought she was being clever, keeping him talking, while she scoped out the shower room, hoping to pick up the faint illumination of an emergency exit, but it was hopeless. This was the basement and there was no escape, but she could still let everyone know where she was. What was happening. If only she could convince him that she wasn't going to make a run for it so he'd leave her to get dressed...

She shook her head. 'It doesn't matter. My name is Lucy, by the way. Lucy Bright. But you already know that.'

'I caught the Lucy on the news. Not the Bright. It explains the B in Lucy B.'

News?

That hideous scene had been on the news? Well, of course it had. The unveiling of the new look for his fashion chain, taking it upmarket, providing aspirational clothes for the career-minded woman. Clothes for work and play.

Clothes with a touch of class and a fair trade label was a big story. Providing new jobs both here and in the Third World.

'How d'you do, Lucy Bright?' he said, finally removing his hand from her arm and offering it to her.

She clutched the towel with one hand, placed her other in his, watching as his long fingers and broad palm swallowed up her own small hand. A rush of warmth warned her she was doing the head to toe blush again.

'To be honest, I've had better days, Nathaniel Hart.'

'Maybe I can help. Why don't you get dressed and then we'll go and see what's good in the Food Hall? I'm sure I can find something more enticing than crisps and chocolate for your supper.'

What?

'There is nothing more enticing than crisps and chocolate.'

Healthier, maybe, but right now she was in the market for high carb, high calorie comfort food.

'And we do need to discuss your camping arrangements,' he continued, ignoring the interruption, 'because, even if you manage to evade the security cameras, I'm afraid the cleaners will spot you.'

'They clean inside the tents?'

'That's probably a push of the vacuum too far,' he admitted, 'but they will certainly notice one zipped up from the inside. You don't imagine you're the first person to have that idea, do you?' He didn't wait for her answer. 'Take your time. No rush,' he said, surrendering her arm, leaving a cold spot where his hand had been, using it to take a phone from his pocket as he turned and walked away, finally leaving her to get dressed.

* * *

Appointments...
20:00 Camping out for the night in H&H outdoors
department.
20:30 Or maybe not.

Nat finished his call, then leaned back against the wall
opposite the locker room door and waited, closing his eyes
in an attempt to block out the image that was indelibly
imprinted upon his mind.

Lucy Bright backing naked out of the shower stall, water
pouring off her shoulders, back, the deliciously soft curve
of her backside. Her determined chin as she'd faced him
down despite the hot pink flush that had spread just about
everywhere.

Her struggle not to smile, when a smile would, undoubtedly, have been in her best interests.

A drop of water sliding slowly around a curl released
from its airy hold, hanging for a moment before it finally
fell. Lying for a moment in the hollow above her collarbone
before it was joined by another and had gathered sufficient
weight to overcome inertia and trickle down between her
breasts.

Smooth shoulders lifted in the merest shrug as she ad-
opted a carelessly casual response to the awkwardness of
the situation.

Like a swan, all appeared serene on the surface, while
her brain had clearly been whirring like the freewheeling
cogs of a machine as she tried to engage gear and figure
out how to escape him for a second time. Work out her next
move.

Or maybe his.

Good question. What exactly *was* he going to do?

Until five minutes ago, he'd thought it was simple. He

would deliver her to friends and walk away. No more, no less complicated than driving Pam home this afternoon.

But it wasn't simple. Simple had become a fantasy from the moment he'd touched her, looked into her green-gold eyes. From the moment he'd glimpsed her luscious curves.

While his head was demanding that he call a cab, dump her in it and send her on her way, do what he could to help without getting involved, his heart—mostly his heart—wasn't having any of it.

That foolish organ demanded that he scoop her up, carry her to his apartment and keep her safe from harm.

Neither was an option.

It was clear that she didn't trust him further than she could throw him, and why would she? In her shoes, he'd be expecting the police to arrive at any minute to remove her from the premises.

What he had to do was keep his head, keep his distance—despite arms aching to wrap her up, keep her safe—but, most important of all, keep her from running.

He had no idea what had caused the row with Rupert Henshawe, or why he'd sent his heavies after her, but he did know that while she was here, under his roof, no harm would come to her. And that, he told himself, was all that mattered.

He looked at the shoe he was still holding, hoping that without it she'd think twice about making a dash for it the first chance she got.

Not so easy with the store closed but she was right, she was smart and, like the involvement issue, he wasn't banking on it.

We?

Lucy caught sight of herself in one of the mirrors and snapped her jaw shut. For a moment there she'd almost succumbed to the fantasy that he might be a good guy.

Perhaps the atmosphere in the grotto was rubbing off on her and, like the little girl in the lift, she wanted to believe.

Had they seen that in her? Rupert's PR people. The longing for something that had always been out of reach. Not the glamour, the clothes, but something deeper. A need for love so desperate that she would be emotionally seduced by the fairy tale of the beast tamed by the innocent.

In other words, a sucker.

Because only an idiot would have fallen for it. She knew she wasn't special. Not tall and elegant or the slightest bit gorgeous. She wasn't an 'It' girl, or a model, or an actress. Nothing like the kind of woman billionaires were usually seen with. Not the kind of woman Rupert had dated in droves—even while remaining determinedly uncommitted—before he'd apparently been bowled over by her innocent charms.

So innocent that he'd insisted on waiting until they were married before they moved their relationship beyond a few kisses.

How many women would have been dumb enough to fall for *that* fairy tale?

Forget the still small voice in the back of her head. The fact that he found it so easy to resist temptation, the fact that she was perfectly happy to go along with it, wasn't panting with frustration, should have sent not just warning bells clanging but klaxons wailing an ear-splitting warning.

It was so obvious, faced with reality, that she was in love with the idea of being in love, the fairy tale, rather than the man. While Rupert...

Well, his motives were clear enough.

He could have paid a celebrity to be the face, the figure

to relaunch his fashion chain, but he wanted a real woman who he would transform with his new 'look'. An ordinary woman.

Apparently she was a breath of fresh air. Real. That was how the PR people had described her in their report. Not a model or a star, but someone who every women in their sales demographic would instantly relate to, aspire to be. Would believe.

So far, so simple. And the rest of it had started as a throwaway line scribbled in the margins of a report.

And she'd fallen for it, believed him, because it had never once occurred to her that it was all a big fat lie. What, for heaven's sake, would be the point of that?

Innocent was right.

The point, of course, was money. A lot of money. Now she knew the truth, she could bring the whole edifice crashing down. It would cost him millions and he wasn't about to let that happen.

She dug out her phone and with shaky fingers she keyed in a tweet while she had a chance.

Lies, lies, lies...

She stopped. There was no signal. Had she been cut off? Or was it just because she was in the deepest part of the basement, surrounded by concrete? She'd had one a couple of hours ago by the coffee machine...

It didn't matter. Whatever the cause, she was, for the moment at least, totally on her own.

Nothing new there. She'd been on her own for most of her life. And if she was trembling by the time she tugged a comb through her damp hair it was with anger rather than fear.

She was absolutely furious with Rupert for lying to

her, with Nathaniel Hart for making her want to believe him, but most of all with herself for being so gullible, so stupid.

Diary update: Everything was going so well. I was safe for the night. All I had to do was keep my head down, stay out of the way of security patrols and I was home dry. Well, wet, actually, because I couldn't resist taking a shower...

Oh, for goodness' sake, she thought, closing the phone. What was the point?

She was up the creek without a paddle and going nowhere. At least not for the moment. Once she was out of the basement all bets were off, but for now the best she could do was get dressed and be ready to take advantage of the slightest opportunity.

She lifted the towel from her shoulders and began vigorously rubbing at her hair. The last thing she needed was pneumonia. In fact... She gave up on the hair and sorted through the pile of discarded elf clothes, picking out the tights, bootees and even the hat, pushing them into the depths of her bag.

The bootees weren't going to be snow-proof, but they would be a lot better than bare feet.

Guilt warred with a sense of triumph as she finished towelling herself off. Triumph won as she stepped into fragile lacy underwear which would do nothing to keep the cold out. She fastened her bra and then reached for her dress.

Her hand met the bare slats of the bench and she turned to look.

Her dress, along with the towel tossed aside by Nathaniel Hart, had slipped to the floor.

She made a wild grab for it but both dress and towel had been lying there quite long enough to soak up water like a sponge and, as she lifted it from the floor, it dripped icy-cold water down her legs.

In desperation she squeezed it. Rolled it up in a dry towel. The towel got wet. The dress did not get noticeably drier.

It was the elf costume or nothing.

She groaned. She might be in a mess but the dress did things to her figure that the elf costume could never hope to achieve. She *knew* what effect the dress had on Nathaniel Hart. Wearing that, she had a chance of distracting him but, while her underwear would have undoubtedly done the job with bells on, she could hardly make her escape in a couple of scraps of lace.

Too late to do any good, she moved to the far end of the bench where it was dry and climbed back into the only warm clothes she possessed. The elf suit. The gorgeous stripy green tights. The tunic that was a little too tight. The neat little belt with the pouch to keep her acorns in. Or whatever it was that elves ate. The flat, floppy around the ankles bootees.

Terrific.

At least she could put on some make-up. And she wasn't talking about freckles.

Five minutes later, lips pink, eyes smudgy, blusher discreetly applied and her damp hair released from the iron grip of hair straighteners and curling ridiculously around her head, she tugged on the tunic and sighed.

This was so not a good look. Her only hope was that some persistent paparazzo would snatch a snap of her leaving the store, being bundled into Rupert's car.

Or did that come under the realms of fantasy, too? There was an underground car park and that was where he'd pick her up, out of sight. Drive her away in a car with blacked-out windows. Or just shoved to the floor out of sight. No need for pretence.

She gathered her coat and bag, scared but determined not to let it show. Then, with her hand on the door, she paused. She still had the file and that gave her an edge. Bargaining power. Removing it from her bag, she stowed it in an empty locker, then looked around for a place to hide the key.

Once that was done, there was nothing more she could do but face the music—or, more accurately, the deliciously elegant Nathaniel Hart.

She gave one more tug on the hem of the tunic, reminding herself that it could be worse—at least she was wearing more than a damp towel. Actually, come to think of it, that might not be…

No. Telling herself to behave, be brave—she had more to worry about than how she looked—she took a deep breath and opened the door.

No poker face this time.

Between the elf costume and her wet hair sticking out at all angles, it was not her finest fashion hour, at least if the eyebrow gymnastics were anything to go by.

Making the most of a bad job, she pasted on a bright smile and gave him a twirl. 'What do you think?' she asked. 'Does my bum look big in this?'

There was a long moment—too long–while he considered the matter and her smile began to wobble. What kind of idiot drew attention to her worst bits?

'What happened to your dress?' he finally asked, avoiding her question.

'Are you referring to the world's most expensive floor cloth?' she responded, giving herself a mental slap for asking a question to which she already knew the answer.

'I don't know. Am I?'

'The dress that some idiot man managed to knock into a freezing puddle with a badly tossed towel?' She didn't wait for him to answer that one. 'You don't think I'd be wearing this if there was any choice, do you?'

'You were happy enough to grab it this afternoon,' he reminded her, 'although I have admit that it is rather—'

She glared at him, daring him to say the word *tight*.

'—green.' He opened the door that led into the electrical department. 'It goes with your eyes,' he added, taking her elbow as he fell in beside her. Not in a frog-marching way. Just a touch, a guiding hand, rather like a gentleman escorting a lady in to dinner in some Jane Austen movie, but she wasn't fooled by that. Or his attempt at gallantry. She knew he was simply keeping contact so that if she decided to make a run for it all he had to do was tighten his grip.

She'd do it, too, at the first chance of escape.

For the moment, however, she forced herself to relax so that she wouldn't telegraph her intentions. She'd already witnessed the lightning speed of his reactions when he'd stopped her from falling on the stairs. Lightning in every sense of the word. That moment while something seemed to fuse between them had been like a lightning strike. For a moment they had both been a little dazed. She wasn't dazed now, though—well, not much—and carrying her kicking and screaming through the store was an entirely different kettle of fish. And if she decided to play hide and seek she might be able to hold out until morning.

Not so easy when the store was empty. There were cameras everywhere. But that worked both ways. His security people, the ones he'd warned her about, would be watching...

She realised that he was looking at her.

'What?' she demanded.

'Nothing. I was just speculating on Frank Alyson's response to the liberties you've taken with your elf costume.' He sounded grave, but a smile was tugging at the corner of his mouth. 'Your belt is a little too tight and your make-up is definitely non-regulation. Where are the rosy cheeks and freckles?' he asked. 'And you must know that you're improperly dressed without your hat.'

Okay, he was teasing and, despite everything, she was sorely tempted to smile. Instead, she reminded herself that they were *his* security people. They would believe whatever he told them and she couldn't deny that she was on the premises illegally.

Cool. She had to play it cool. Wait her chance.

'So…what? He'll feed me to the troll?'

'Troll?' he asked, startled into a grin and set off a whole new wave of sparks flaring through her body.

Maybe she could set off a fire alarm, she thought desperately, doing her best to ignore them. Or there were the cleaners. They would be arriving soon; he'd said so. They had to get in. And get out again.

'It's what he does to underachieving elves,' she replied, deadpan. 'But I'm off duty so I'm afraid you're going to have to live with "improper", at least until my dress dries,' she said, as if her clothing disaster was the only thing on her mind. 'Always supposing it survives the dunking.'

'I'm sorry about the dress. For some reason I didn't notice it.'

Well, no. He'd been too busy not noticing her towel slipping all over the place…

'I'll replace it, of course.'

'It was a one-off. A designer original.'

'Oh. Well, let's hope it dries out.'

'It had better. Everything else I own is packed up in a couple of boxes. Along with my life.'

The life she'd had before she met Rupert Henshawe. It hadn't been very exciting, but it had been real. Honest. Truthful.

Her clothes, including the most expensive suit she'd ever bought, the one she'd bought for her interview at the Henshawe Corporation—she'd been so determined to make a good impression. It had done its job, but of course it hadn't been good enough for Lucy B.

There was an ancient laptop she'd bought second-hand. All the letters were worn off the keys but it had seen her through her business course. A box of books for her college work. A few precious memories from her childhood.

She'd left pretty much everything else behind when the constant presence of the media on the doorstep of the tiny flat she'd shared with two other girls had made it impossible to do even the simplest thing. When even a trip to the corner shop for a bottle of milk had become a media scrum.

Her kettle, radio, her crocks and pots. The bits and pieces she'd accumulated since she'd left the care system.

She was now worse off than she'd ever been. No job, nowhere to live. She was going to have to start again from scratch.

How much did she have left in her old account? Enough for the deposit on a room in a flat share?

There had been a time when she'd have known to the last penny.

'I didn't plan this very well, did I?' she said, trying to keep the panic out of her voice.

'I've no idea what you've done, Lucy.'

Nothing. She hadn't done a thing...

'I missed the start of the news bulletin but you wield a mean handbag.'

'That man grabbed me,' she protested. 'He wouldn't let me go.'

'I wasn't criticising. It must have been terrifying to be caught up in that kind of media mayhem. I didn't catch the wrap up,' he prompted. 'As you're aware, Pam collapsed and I was called away.'

'Is she going to be okay?' Lucy asked.

'Just a seasonal bug. She should have stayed at home, but it tends to get hectic at this time of year.'

She glanced at him. 'You saw me, didn't you? When you were talking to Mr Alyson.'

'I saw the costume,' he said. 'Not you. I was looking for a girl in a very sexy black dress.'

At least he didn't deny that he'd been looking for her.

'It was only later,' he added, glancing down at her, 'when I remembered your beauty spot, that I realised it was you.'

'My what?'

'Your beauty spot,' he repeated, pausing, turning to face her. 'Here.'

'That's not…'

Her voice dried as he touched his fingertip to the corner of her lip. He was close, his eyes were dark, slumberous as he looked down at her, and for a moment she thought he was going to kiss her, finish what he'd started on the stairs.

Her heart rate picked up, hammering in her throat; all she could see was his mouth, bracketed by a pair of deep lines and, as his lower lip softened, she finally understood the depth of Rupert's betrayal. Just how shockingly she had been fooled. Because this was how it should be. The entire body engaged, every cell focused on the desire for the touch, the taste of that mouth against hers. Nothing else. And, as a finger of heat spiralled through her, a tiny, urgent gasp escaped her lips.

The sound, barely audible, was enough to shatter the spell. He raised heavy lids, lifting his gaze from her mouth to her eyes and dropped his hand.

'It's j-just a mole,' she said quickly, taking a step back, putting an arm's length between them before straightening her shoulders, lifting her chin. 'Rupert wanted me to have it removed. Just a little bit too warts-and-all ordinary for him, apparently.'

'If Henshawe thinks you're ordinary he needs to get his eyes tested.'

'Does he?' she asked, for a moment distracted by the unexpected compliment. But only for a moment. 'Well, green striped tights do tend to make you stand out from the crowd,' she said in an attempt at carelessness that she was a long way from feeling. And then wished she hadn't as he gave her legs the kind of attention that they could do without at the moment.

'True,' he said, finally dragging his gaze away from them, 'but I noticed you before you morphed into an elf,' he reminded her as he retrieved her elbow and headed briskly for the stairs.

'It's hard to miss someone falling over their own feet right in front of you,' she said, stumbling a little in the soft boots as she struggled to keep up with him.

He slowed, a consideration that she was sure neither Rupert nor his men would show her.

'Of course I have spent the last few months being buffed and polished and waxed,' she rushed on, trying not to think about how much 'notice' he'd taken of her. How close he'd just come to 'noticing' her again—this time in an empty store with none of the constraints of shoppers pounding past them. He was the enemy, for heaven's sake, and while she wanted to throw him off the scent, she wasn't entirely sure who would be distracting who... 'My hair has been streaked, my eyelashes dyed, my eyebrows threaded and I've lost weight, too.'

'Don't tell me. You had a personal trainer.'

'Good grief, no. I've just been too busy to snack between meals.' She gave him an arch look, ran a finger over one of her well-tended brows. 'You have no idea how much time it takes to look this groomed.'

He glanced at her, taking a long look at her messy hair and clothes that not even a catwalk model could make look good.

'Forget I said that,' she said hurriedly. 'I've been deprived of chocolate for too long and it's affecting my brain.'

Suddenly desperate for the instant gratification of chocolate melting on the tongue, she stopped, forcing him to do the same, dug the chocolate finger biscuit out of her elf pouch—so much more satisfying than acorns—and unwrapped it. As she raised it to her mouth she realised that she had an audience and she snapped it in half, offering one of the fingers to Nathaniel Hart.

He shook his head, not bothering to hide a smile. And she was right. The distraction was mutual. 'Your need is greater.'

She wasn't arguing and she bit into it, struggling to contain a groan of sheer pleasure.

'Better?'

'Marginally. Don't get me wrong,' she said, licking her fingers—she'd been carrying the chocolate next to her body and it was soft. 'I enjoyed it all. The gorgeous clothes. Being made over, every single bit of me being made as perfect as humanly possible without the intervention of surgery. Who wouldn't?'

That, after all, was the dream she was selling. Buy your clothes from this store and you too can have all this.

'Surgery?'

'I drew the line at the boob job. And the spray tan. I like my orange in a glass. Or chocolate-flavoured.'

She tossed a glance in his direction, but he shook his head. 'No comment.'

'Oh, please. Everyone has an opinion.' From the editor of a magazine who was desperate to do a step-by-step photo feature of a silicone implant—and had really struggled to hide her annoyance when she'd refused to play along—to the woman who did her nails. Everyone, apparently, wanted a bigger cup size. Everyone except her. She put her hands to her waist and pushed out her chest, straining the buttons to the limit. 'Apparently my naturalness and lack of guile wasn't, when push came to shove, quite enough. But that's the Cinderella story, isn't it? She had to be transformed before she was fit for the prince. All imperfections disappearing with a wave of a magic wand. Or the modern equivalent.'

He lifted an eyebrow.

'Photoshop.'

'But he still wanted her when he saw her as she really was. In her rags and covered with ashes from the hearth.'

'Oh, please! He didn't even recognise her.' She looked at the elegant red suede shoe he was still carrying, then up at Nathaniel Hart. 'Do you want to risk it?' she asked. 'If the shoe doesn't fit, will you let me go?'

'The shoe fell out of your bag, Lucy.'

'Did you see it fall?'

'Well, no...'

'Then I believe that is what's known in legal circles as circumstantial evidence.'

'Not if I find the matching one in there.'

'The matching one is jammed in a grating two streets away.' Then, unable to bear the suspense, the teasing pretence a moment longer, 'Shall we cut the pretence? How long have I got?'

His dark brows drew together in a puzzled frown. 'I'm sorry? How long have you got for what?'

'There's no need to pretend. I know you've called him. Rupert,' she added when his frown only deepened. 'I saw you. As you left the locker room.'

'The only person I've spoken to in the last twenty minutes—apart from you—is my chief security officer. To inform him that, rather than going straight to my office, I was still in the store.'

They'd reached the Food Hall and he released her elbow, snagged a trolley and headed down the nearest aisle.

Not Rupert?

Lucy firmly smothered the little flicker of hope that he was for real, ate the second finger of biscuit for comfort and went after him.

'Nice try,' she said when she caught up, 'but you were following me. On the stairs.'

'We were going in the same direction,' he conceded, picking up a box of eggs, glancing back at her. 'What made you look back?'

'Sheer paranoia? When I ran out of that hotel I had a dozen or so people on my tail. I knew I wasn't far enough ahead to have evaded all of them. I was trying not to draw attention to myself,' she said. 'Waiting for the hand on my shoulder.'

'And you thought I was the hand?'

'Aren't you? I heard you tell Frank Alyson to keep a

look out...' She faltered as he stopped by a shelf containing breakfast cereals. She was beginning to sound paranoid. Could she have got it wrong? That he didn't have a clue what she was talking about...'You will tell me if I'm making a total idiot of myself, won't you?'

CHAPTER SIX

'YOU'RE making a total idiot of yourself,' Nathaniel said obligingly, 'but it's okay. You're scared. I don't know why and you don't have to tell me. And I had the people following you escorted from the store.'

'You did? But how did you know?'

'They weren't discreet.' The muscles in his jaw tightened momentarily. 'Of course it's likely they were replaced but you should be safe enough now that the store is closed. They'll have to accept that you aren't inside and go away.' He continued to examine the shelf. 'Be glad to in this weather, I should think.'

'I suppose.'

'As for me, I was just doing my afternoon round of the store. It was pure chance that I happened to be following you up the stairs. What's your favourite cereal?' he asked, looking back at her.

'Mr Hart...'

'Nat. This one looks interesting,' he said, taking a box from the shelf. 'It has fruit pieces and something called clusters.'

'Nathaniel...'

'What are "clusters"?'

'Not one of your five-a-day,' she snapped, beginning to lose it. No. She'd lost it the minute he'd looked at her. He was looking at her now and her mouth dried. 'I haven't the faintest idea. I've never bought fancy breakfast cereals in my life. I always have porridge.'

'Always?'

'It's cheap, filling and good for you.' And, even when you had a platinum credit card with your name on it, old habits died hard.

'It also requires a saucepan and heat,' he pointed out.

'I was quite content with the crisps and the chocolate.'

'You've eaten the chocolate,' he reminded her, replacing the fancy cereal with its fruit and clusters on the shelf. 'Porridge it is.'

'No! I don't want anything.'

But he'd tossed a smart tartan box into the trolley.

It bore about as much similarity to the jumbo pack of own-brand oats she bought from the supermarket as the Lucy B version of the cashmere dress she'd abandoned, and she was sure the packaging reflected the price.

'And, just so there's no misunderstanding,' he continued, scanning the shelves as they moved on, 'the only thing I was asking Frank to keep an eye open for was anyone else showing signs of the bug that laid Pam low.'

'But—'

'The last thing I need at this time of year is an epidemic. Staff passing it on to the children visiting the grotto.'

She looked up at him, searched his face. He submitted patiently to her scrutiny, as if he understood what she was doing. He looked genuine but so had everyone else she'd met in the last few months. All those nice people who had been lying to her.

She could no longer trust her own judgement.

'Can I believe you?'

'It doesn't really matter what I say, does it? If I've called Henshawe to tell him where you are there is no escape. If

I haven't, then you're safe. Only time can set your mind at rest.'

'So,' she asked, a wry smile pulling at her lip, 'is that a yes or a no?'

His only response was to reach for a bottle of maple syrup and add it to the trolley.

'Suppose I insisted on leaving?' she persisted. 'Right this minute.'

'I'd find you some warm clothes and then drive you wherever you wanted to go.'

'Why?'

'Because, interesting though that outfit is, I imagine you'd rather leave wearing something that doesn't look as if you've escaped from a pantomime.'

Lucy discovered that she couldn't speak.

'Because you're under my roof, Lucy. Staff, temp, customer, you're my responsibility.'

She shook her head in disbelief.

'You're afraid I'd trick you? That I'd take you to him?'

He didn't appear to take offence which, considering the way she'd been casting doubt on his character, was suspicious in itself and Lucy shook her head again. Her entire world had been turned upside down for the second time in months, but this time not for the good.

'I can't trust anyone. I thought I knew Rupert. I thought he cared for me. I don't and he doesn't. The only thing he appears to care about is his profit and loss statement.'

'Are you sure? I don't know Henshawe, other than by reputation,' he continued when she didn't say anything. 'What I've read in the financial pages. Frankly, he's not a man I'd want to do business with, but love can change a man.'

'Well, that's just rubbish and you know it,' she declared.

'The only time you can change a man is when he's in nappies.'

She saw him pull his lips back tight against his teeth, doing his best not to smile. His eyes let him down.

'It's not funny!' But she found herself struggling with a giggle. 'Rupert Henshawe is not, and never was, in love with me. What we had was not a romance, I discovered today, but a marketing campaign. That's why I gave him back his ring.'

'A masterpiece in understatement, if I might say so. You have a good throwing arm, by the way. Have you ever played cricket?'

'They showed that on the news?' She groaned, mortified at the spectacle she'd made of herself. Then she sighed. 'What does it matter? It'll be on the front page of every newspaper tomorrow morning. The only story about our relationship that wasn't carefully stage-managed by his PR team.'

'You and the PR team got lucky. Tomorrow's headlines will all be about the weather.'

'It's still snowing?'

'Deep and crisp and even,' he said. 'Traffic chaos from one end of the country to the other. It's no night for an elf to be out.' He paused. 'Especially not in something that doesn't cover her—'

'I've got the picture.' She tugged on the back of the tunic. 'Thank you.'

When she still didn't move he took her hand and pressed his phone, warm from his pocket, into it.

'If you can't trust me, take this, call Enquiries and ask for a cab firm, although I warn you you'll have a long wait in this weather.'

Calling her bluff. He knew she had nowhere to go. She

opened it, anyway. Keyed in the number for Enquiries but, before it was answered, she broke the connection.

'We both know that if I had anywhere to go, anyone to call, I wouldn't be standing here in this ridiculous outfit,' she said. 'I'd be long gone.'

Nat watched her accept the bitter truth and felt his heart breaking for her. No one should be so alone. So friendless.

'I'm sorry. It's tough when you love someone and they let you down.'

'Love is a word, not an emotion, Nathaniel. We're sold on it from the time we're old enough to listen to fairy tales. Songs, movies, books… It's a marketing man's dream. I was in love with the idea of being in love, that's all. Swept up in the Cinderella story as much as anyone buying the latest issue of *Celebrity*. It's not my heart that's in a mess. It's my life.' About to hand the phone back to him, she said, 'Actually, would you mind if I sent a message?'

'You've thought of someone?'

Why didn't that make him feel happier?

'Half a million someones,' she replied. 'My Twitter and Facebook followers. Some of them must be genuine.'

'It seems a fair bet,' he admitted. 'What will you say?'

'Don't worry, I'm not about to ask them to descend en masse on Hastings & Hart and rescue me.'

'Pity. It would make this the best Christmas H&H have ever had,' he said, then wished he hadn't.

'Sorry. While I'd like to oblige you by delivering a store full of customers at opening time, right now I'm doing my best to stay beneath the radar while I figure out what to do.'

'It's your call. What will you say?'

'*Trust no one*…springs to mind. Or does that sound a touch paranoid?'

'Just a touch.' He turned away, giving her a moment to think while he pretended to scan the shelf. 'And since Henshawe, in his statement to camera regarding your outburst, managed to imply that you not only had an eating disorder but were mainlining tranquillisers to deal with the stress of your new lifestyle, that might not be in your best interests.'

'He did *what?*'

'He was touchingly sincere.'

Her eyes narrowed.

'I'm just saying. Having met you, I can see how unlikely that is. At least about the eating disorder,' he added, tossing a packet of chocolate biscuits into the trolley. The ones with really thick chocolate and orange cream in the middle. Maybe they'd tempt her to stay.

'Thanks for that!'

Lucy noted the chocolate biscuits. The man was not just eye candy. He paid attention…

'Any time. And, let's face it, you're a bit too sparky to be on tranquillisers.'

'Sparky?' She grinned. Couldn't help herself. '*Sparky?*'

'I was being polite.'

'Barely,' she suggested. 'You're right, of course. It was my mouth that got me into all this trouble in the first place. But I can see how his mind is working and that does scare me.' And, just like that, she lost all desire to smile.

'He blamed the press for causing the problems by hounding you out of the flat you shared with your friends.'

'If you're attempting to reassure me, I have to tell you that it's not working.'

'You didn't feel hounded?'

Nat added some crackers to the trolley, then crossed

to the cold cabinet and began to load up with milk, juice, salads, cheese.

'A bit,' she admitted, trailing after him. 'I couldn't move without a lens in my face, but since it was his PR people who were orchestrating the hysteria it seems a bit rich to blame the poor saps wielding the cameras. But I have fair warning what to expect when Rupert catches up with me.'

Nat glanced at her.

'I'll be whisked into one of his fancy clinics for my own good,' she said, responding to his unasked question.

'He has clinics?'

'He has a finger in all kinds of businesses, including a chain of clinics that provides every comfort to the distressed celebrity. A nip and tuck while you're drying out?' she said, pulling on her cheeks to stretch her mouth. 'No problem. A little Botox to smooth away the excesses of a coke habit? Step right in. Once he's got me there, he'll probably throw away the key.'

Lucy attempted a careless laugh, but he suspected that she was trying to convince herself rather more than him that she was joking.

He was more concerned why Henshawe would want her out of the way that badly—or why she'd think he would—and when he didn't join in she stopped pretending and frowned at the phone.

'How about, *I'll be back!*...?' she offered.

'Will you?' he asked. 'Go back?'

'To Rupert?' She appeared puzzled. 'Why would I do that?'

'Because that's what women do.'

'You think this is just some tiff?' she demanded when he didn't answer. 'That it'll blow over once I've straightened myself out? Got my head together?'

'It happens,' he said, pushing her, hoping that she might volunteer some answers.

'Not in this case.'

She snapped the phone shut without sending any kind of message and offered it back to him.

'Why don't you hang on to it for now?' he suggested. 'In case you change your mind.'

She looked at him, still unsure of his motives. Then she shrugged, tucked the phone into the pouch at her belt.

'Thanks.'

Her voice was muffled, thick, and he turned away, picked up a couple of apples and dropped them in the trolley. Giving her a moment. Sparky she might be, but no one could fail to be affected by a bad breakup. Especially one that had been played out in the full gaze of the media. Tears were inevitable.

After a moment she picked up a peach, weighed it in her hand, sniffed it. Replaced it.

'No good?' he asked, taking one himself to check it for ripeness.

'They are a ridiculous price.'

'I can probably manage if you really want one. I get staff discount.'

That teased a smile out of her, but she shook her head. 'Peaches are summer fruit. They need to be warm.'

And, just like that, he could see her sitting in the shade of an Italian terrace, grapes ripening overhead, her teeth sinking into the flesh of a perfectly ripe sun-warmed peach straight from the tree. Bare shoulders golden, meltingly relaxed.

Her lips glistening, sweet with the juice…

'I get why you ran out of the press conference, Lucy,' he said, crushing the image with cold December reality. 'But, having dumped the man so publicly, I don't understand why he's so desperate to find you.'

She swallowed, managed a careless shrug. 'I thought you didn't want to know.'

He didn't. If he knew, he would be part of it, part of her story. But, conversely, he did, desperately, want her to trust him and the two were intertwined.

'I have something of his. Something he wants back,' she admitted.

The file, he thought, remembering the glossy black ring binder she'd been holding up in the news clip. That she'd been carrying in her bag.

It wasn't there now, he realised.

'Maybe you should just give it back,' he suggested. 'Walk away.'

'I can't do that.'

Before he could ask her why, what she'd done with it, she was distracted by the sound of voices coming through the arch that led to the butchery.

'It's just one of the cleaning crews,' he said quickly, seizing her wrist as panic flared in her face and she turned, hunting for the nearest escape route. 'Good grief, you're shaking like a leaf. What the hell has he done to you? Do you need the police?'

'No!' Her throat moved as she swallowed.

'Are you sure? What about this?' he demanded, releasing her wrist, lifting his hand to skim his fingertips lightly over the bruise darkening at her temple.

She stared at him. 'What? No! A photographer caught me with his camera. It was an accident. Nothing to do with Rupert.' She looked anxiously towards the archway, the voices were getting nearer. 'Please...'

'Okay.' He wasn't convinced—he'd heard every variation of the bruise excuse going—but this wasn't the moment to press it. 'We're done here,' he said, heading for the nearest lift.

'You can't take the trolley out of the food hall,' she protested as the doors opened.

'You want to stay and pack the groceries into carriers?' he asked, stopping them from closing with his foot.

A burst of song propelled her into the lift. 'No, you're all right.'

'Doors closing. Going up...'

'What?' She turned on him. 'Where are you taking me?'

'Believe me, you'll be a lot safer on the top floor than the bottom one,' he said quickly. 'There'll be no security staff. No curious cleaners wondering why you look familiar. Where they've seen you before.'

She opened her mouth, closed it again, her jaw tightening as she swallowed down whatever she was going to say.

'You'd never have got away with it, Lucy.'

'You don't know that,' she declared, staring straight ahead. 'And it would test your security staff. If they found me you'd know they're as good as you think they are.'

'Believe me, they are. And you'd spend the night in a police cell.'

'Oh, but—'

'They don't call me when they find intruders, Lucy. They call the local police station and then the game would be up. If you're so sure that the cleaners would recognise you, I think it's a fair bet to assume that whoever turned up to arrest you would, too.'

She slumped back against the side of the lift. 'You're right, of course. And the elf costume would confirm everything that Rupert was saying about me. That I'm one sandwich short of a picnic.'

'It wouldn't look good,' he agreed. 'But if you really do have your heart set on spending the night in a tent, I'll go and fetch one of those pop-up ones. You can set it up on the bedroom floor.'

The lift came to a halt. *'Tenth floor... Customer services. Accounts. Doors opening...'*

'Bedroom floor?' She frowned. 'I thought the bedroom department was on the fifth...'

She stopped, blushing, remembering too late how she knew that.

'Forget the bedroom department,' he said, leading the way past the customer services department, down a corridor past empty offices. 'Have you never heard of living over the shop?'

'Over the corner shop, maybe,' she said as he used a swipe card to open a door that led to an internal lobby containing a private lift from the car park and a pair of wide double doors. 'But not...'

He keyed a number into a security pad, opened the door and, as he stood back to allow her to precede him, her protest died away.

Ahead of her was the most striking room Lucy had ever seen. Acres of limed floor. A pair of huge square black leather sofas. Starkly modern black and steel furniture. Dove-grey walls. No paintings, no colour, not a single thing to distract from the view through the soaring wall of glass in front of her. Constant movement, the ever-changing vibrant colour of the cityscape against the monochrome room.

'Wow!' she exclaimed, gazing out over a London lit up and laid out at her feet like fairyland. 'You actually live here?' she asked, moving closer.

There were lights everywhere.

Not just the Christmas lights, but every famous landmark

floodlit to show it at its best. There was traffic crossing bridges, strings of lights along the Thames. Even the aircraft coming into land, navigation lights winking, added to the drama.

And Christmas trees, everywhere there were Christmas trees.

Big ones in squares, rows of small ones atop buildings, every shape and size in gardens and shining out of windows. The colours reflected in the big soft flakes of snow falling like feathers over the city, settling on parks, covering trees, rooftops. Wiping the world clean.

He hadn't answered and she turned to him, expecting to see him smiling, amused by her totally uncool reaction.

But his face was expressionless.

'When I'm in London,' he said. 'There are stores all over the country, as well as abroad. I seem to spend a lot of time in hotels.'

'They don't all have apartments like this on the top floor?'

'No. I can say with confidence that this is unique. It was commissioned by my cousin, Christopher Hart, as part of the refurbishment of the Hastings & Hart flagship store.'

'It's amazing. I bet you can't wait to get home.'

'This isn't home...' He bit off the words as if they'd escaped before he could stop them. And when she waited for him to tell her why, 'It's a long story.'

'Is it? Well, here's the deal. You tell me yours and I'll tell you mine.'

'Long and very boring. Make yourself at...'

'Home?' she offered, filling the gap.

He managed a smile. He had an entire repertoire of them, she discovered. Sardonic. Amused. The one that lit up her insides, fizz, whoosh, bang, like a New Year firework display.

And then there was this one. The blank-eyed kind you cranked up when you didn't want anyone to know how you were really feeling. The shutters had come down so fast she almost heard them clang, excluding her. And now they were down she knew how much she wanted to go back two minutes.

'Or not,' she said when the silence had gone on for far too long.

'My problem, not yours, Lucy. Look around. Find yourself a room—there are plenty to choose from. I'll be in the kitchen.'

He didn't wait to see if she accepted his invitation, but returned to the trolley, disappeared through a door. Something had touched a raw nerve and while every instinct was urging her to go after him, put her arms around him, kiss it better, he might as well have painted a sign saying *keep out* on his back.

Instead, she took him at his word and looked around. The small flat she'd occupied at the top of Rupert's townhouse had been elegant, comfortably furnished, but this was real estate on an entirely different level.

It was the kind of apartment that she'd seen featured in the 'at home' features in *Celebrity*. So tidy that it looked as if no one lived there.

This was a somewhat extreme example, she decided. There was no Christmas tree here, no decorations. Not so much as a trace of tinsel.

Maybe, she decided, when you worked with it all day, you needed to escape. Maybe.

This might be a stunning apartment but he'd said himself that it wasn't home. So where was? She wanted to know.

Her fingers trailed over the butter-soft leather of the sofa as she turned, taking it all in and, looking up, she saw an open gallery with the same stunning view of the city. It was reached by a circular staircase and, taking Nathaniel at his word, she went up, finding herself in a space wide enough for casual seating. Armchairs in more of that soft black leather.

There was a single pair of black panelled doors. Assuming that they led to an internal lobby where she'd find the bedrooms, she opened one and stepped through.

For a moment all she could see was the blinking of the navigation lights of a plane passing overhead, then soft concealed lighting, responding to movement, gradually revealed the room she'd stumbled into.

The dark, asymmetrical pyramid of glass above her that would, by day, light the room. The tip of a landmark that rose like a spear into the sky. Silver in the rain. Bronze, gold, fiery red when struck by the sun. Never the same.

Below it was the largest bedroom she had ever seen, perfect in every striking detail. The walls were a soft dove-grey and, apart from the bed, a vast space of pure white, the only furniture was a cantilevered slab of black marble that ran the entire width of the room behind the bed.

Unable to stop herself, she opened a door that led to a pair of dressing and bath rooms. His and hers.

Nathaniel's?

No. Despite an array of the most luxurious toiletries, the designer suits, couturier dresses, in the walk-in wardrobes, it was obvious that neither of them was in use. It wasn't just the fact that all the clothes were cocooned in plastic covers.

There was no presence here. Like the rest of the apartment, it was visually stunning, austere, silent.

But here the silence was a hollow, suffocating emptiness.

Even the art was monochrome. Just one piece, a black-framed architectural impression of the Hastings & Hart building that filled the space above the bed.

The only point of colour in the room was a single crimson rose in a silver bud vase gleaming against the black marble.

She touched a velvety petal, expecting it to be silk, but it was real. The one thing in the room, in the entire apartment, as far as she could tell, that was alive and she shivered as she stared up at the drawing.

The building was a thing of light, energy, leaping from the earth. While this...

'This isn't home...'

And then her eyes focused on the signature on the drawing.

Nathaniel Hart.

Nat emptied the groceries onto the central island of the vast kitchen that he rarely used for anything other than making coffee.

He'd offered to pitch Lucy a tent but wasn't that what he was doing? Camping out. Living here but doing his best not to touch anything.

As if by not making an impression, not disturbing anything, maybe one morning he would wake up and he'd be back in his own life. The nightmare over.

Lucy closed the doors, quietly retraced her steps down to the lower floor, found the kitchen.

Nathaniel was standing with his back to the door, arms spread wide, hands gripping the counter so hard that his knuckles were white. Certain she was intruding, she took an instinctive step backwards, but he heard and half turned, his face as empty as the room upstairs.

'I'm lost,' she said quickly.

'Lost?'

'Not so much lost as confused. I went upstairs. It seemed the obvious thing to do.' She lifted a shoulder in an embarrassed little shrug.

'My fault.' He straightened, dragged both hands through his hair. 'I should have given you the guided tour instead of leaving you to find your own way around.'

'I could have found my own way. I just didn't want to blunder in anywhere else that's private.'

'It's not private. It's just…' He shook his head. 'Come on, I'll show you around.' He grasped her hand and led the way to a wide corridor with a series of doors, all on one side.

'Linen cupboard,' he said, keeping her hand tucked in his. 'Bedroom, bedroom, bedroom…' opening doors to reveal three empty bedrooms, all decorated with the same pale walls, black marble night tables, white linen as the room upstairs. 'Bedroom,' he repeated, opening the last door to reveal yet more of the same, finally releasing her hand, leaving it for her to decide whether or not to follow him inside because this was not just another bedroom.

'This is your room,' she said.

'The master suite upstairs spooked you and you don't know me.' He turned to face her. 'I wanted you to see for yourself that I have nothing to hide.'

'You don't feel like a stranger,' she said, following him, placing her hand in his. Foolish, maybe, especially considering the way her heart leapt whenever he was within ten feet of her. Yes, the room upstairs had spooked her, but it didn't seem to be doing much for him either, and his fingers closed about hers. Almost as if they were uniting against the world.

The word dropped into her chest with a thunk, but for once she kept her mouth closed, her thoughts to herself.

United…

That was what it had felt like when he'd held her on the stairs. Instinctive. Natural. There had been no barriers between them, only an instant and mutual recognition, and in another place somewhere private, they'd have been out of their clothes, not caring about anything but the need to touch, to hold and be held, feel the heat of another human body.

Not just lust at first sight. Something far deeper than that.

Slightly shocked at the direction her mind was taking, she forced herself to retrieve her hand, ignore the cold emptiness where his palm had been pressed against hers and concentrate on the room.

Square, with long, narrow floor to ceiling windows on two sides, it occupied the corner of the building.

Nathaniel had barely made an impression on it. There were a few books piled up on the marble ledge beside the bed and, taking advantage of his invitation, she ran her fingers down the spines. Art. Design. Management. Psychology. No fiction. Nothing just for fun.

The only thing that set this room apart from the others was a drawing board and stool, tucked up into the corner. As far out of the way as possible.

There was nothing else that gave any clue to the man.

A bathroom. A wardrobe-cum-dressing room, smaller than the ones upstairs. At least his clothes were lived in, used and, unable to help herself, she lifted the sleeve of one of maybe a dozen identical white shirts.

She turned, saw that he was watching her. 'Fresh air,' she said. 'It smells of fresh air. Like washing hung out on a windy day.'

'You're wasted as an elf. You should be writing copy for the manufacturers of laundry products.'

'Not me!' She shook her head. 'Sorry, I didn't mean to snap, but I'm right off the whole idea of marketing right now.'

She dropped the sleeve, stepped past him, back into the bedroom.

'Tell me, Nathaniel,' she asked as she looked around, 'did you get a discount for buying in bulk?'

'Bulk?'

'The paint. The marble. I know you designed the building. I saw your drawing. In the room upstairs.'

'I designed the building. The store,' he confirmed. 'But the apartment was private space, decorated to client specification. The idea was that nothing should distract from the windows. The colour, the movement. The concept of the city as living art.'

'Right.'

'You don't like it?'

'The initial impact is stunning. The views are incredible, but...' She hesitated as she struggled to find the words to explain how she felt.

'But?'

'But everything with colour, life, movement is happening somewhere else. To someone else. Up here, you're just...' she gave an awkward little shrug '...a spectator.'

CHAPTER SEVEN

'How long have you been here, Lucy?'

'I don't know. Twenty minutes?' She looked across at him. 'Do you want me to leave now?'

'You're not going anywhere. And I'm not offended. I was merely calculating how long it had taken you to see the fatal flaw in a design that wowed the interior design world. Was featured in a dozen magazines.'

'And was cousin Christopher pleased about that?' she asked, sensing that he wasn't entirely happy with what had been done with the amazing space he'd provided. 'He is the man whose clothes are shrouded in the dressing room upstairs, I take it?'

'He was torn, I'd say. He'd thrown open the doors to the likes of *Celebrity* magazine, wanting the world to see his eyrie. He'd forgotten that I was the one who would be credited with its creation.'

And the impression she'd gained that he didn't like the man much, even if he was kin, solidified.

'I'll bet you a cheese omelette that they all focused on the windows. That's if you'd allow anything that yellow to brighten the monochrome perfection of your kitchen.'

'I let you in,' he reminded her, 'and I promise you no one has ever looked greener, or more out of place.'

'Dressed like this,' she replied, reprising the twirl, 'I'd look out of place anywhere except your basement.'

'True.'

'Maybe you should have left me down there.'

'Maybe you should get out of it.'

Something about the way he was looking at her sent a tremor of longing through her. It was as if something had become unhinged in her brain. Shock—it had to be shock. She didn't do this. But, before she could do something really stupid, she said, 'I think we'll stick with the plan.'

Plan! What plan?

When he didn't answer she crossed to the drawing board to take a look at what he was working on. It wasn't a big project, just the front and side elevations of a single-storey house.

There was a photograph clipped to the corner of the board. Taken from a rocky ledge, the land fell away to a small sandy cove. The site for the house?

The edges of both photograph and drawing were curling slightly, as if they hadn't been touched in a long time. Yet it was here, he kept it close, and she ran a hand over the edge of the photograph in an attempt to smooth it.

'This is nice,' she said, looking back at him. 'Where is it?'

He didn't look at the picture.

'Cornwall.'

'I've never been to Cornwall.'

'You should,' he said, his face devoid of expression and for a moment she thought she'd put her foot in her mouth. Right up to her ankle. 'It's… nice.' Then she saw the tiny betraying flicker at the corner of his eye. 'And full of Cornish piskies. Dressed like that, you'd be right at home.'

He was teasing her?

'I'm not a pixie,' she said, mock indignantly, to disguise the rush of pleasure, warmth, that threatened to overwhelm her. 'I'm an elf.'

'Piskies, not pixies.' Then, abruptly, 'That's the lot. You've seen it all now. Choose a room, Lucy. Make yourself at home. I'll go and make a start on that cheese omelette I owe you.'

'You're admitting I was right?' she demanded, not wanting him to go.

'Smart as paint,' he agreed, leaving her in his room. A gesture of trust? Because she was a stranger, too. Or because he felt the same tug of desire, heat?

Except they weren't. Strangers. They might never have met before but, from the moment their eyes had met, they had known one another, deep down. Responding to something that went far beyond the surface conventions.

She looked again at the photograph.

Nice.

What a pathetic, pitiful word to describe such a landscape. To describe a house designed with such skill that it would become a part of it.

It wasn't *nice*; it was dramatic, powerful, at one with its setting.

It was extraordinary. Twenty minutes. That was all it had taken her to see through surface veneer to the darkness at the heart of the apartment.

He'd designed it as a gift for Claudia, his cousin's wife. Envisaged it filled with light, colour, life—reflecting the light, colour, life of the city. He'd been forced to watch, helpless, as Christopher had taken his vision and sucked the life right out of it. Just as he'd sucked the life right out of the woman he loved.

* * *

Lucy didn't bother to look at each room before deciding which to choose. They were all as soulless as the room upstairs.

She dumped her bag on the bed and checked out the en suite bathroom. Like those upstairs, it was supplied with all the essentials, including a new toothbrush which she fell upon with gratitude.

She'd replace it first thing...

She caught her reflection in the mirror. *First thing* suggested that she was staying. That she had taken him at his word. Trusted that bone-deep connection...

'Not bright, Lucy B,' she said. 'You are such a pushover. One smile and he's got you wrapped around his little finger.'

One look and she'd seen her engagement to Rupert for the sham it was.

But, even if he was as genuine as her instincts—and just how reliable were those dumb whoosh, flash, bang hormones anyway?—were telling her, this was, could only ever be, a very temporary stopgap.

Breathing space.

She took out her own phone and it leapt into life. Of course. Why would Rupert cut her off when it was the one way he could contact her?

There were dozens of voicemails. She ignored them. There was no one she could think of who'd have anything to say that she wanted to hear. But she opened Rupert's last message:

Henshawe 20:12. We need to talk.

Blunt and to the point, it didn't escape her that he'd waited until the store was closed, all the doors were locked and there was no chance that she was still inside before calling her.

Proof, if she needed it, that he'd had someone watching all that time, just in case.

No doubt he'd had everyone out checking anywhere else she might have taken cover, too. She guessed some of the messages were from her former flatmates, the owner of the nursery where she'd worked. Everyone who had touched her life since the day her mother had abandoned her.

No apology, but at least there was no pretence. Forced to accept that she'd somehow slipped through his fingers, he was ready to talk.

The problem there was that there was nothing he had to say that she wanted to hear.

Or maybe one thing, and that was unintentional.

Not that, in her heart of hearts, she'd needed confirmation that Nathaniel really was on the level. That he'd seen she was in trouble and hadn't hesitated to step forward.

That he was one of the good guys.

But it was good to know that her judgement wasn't terminally damaged. Not as crap as she'd thought.

She logged into Twitter. There were hundreds of messages now. And a new hashtag: *#findLucyB*

No prizes for guessing who'd come up with that one, she thought, as she logged into her diary.

Nathaniel Hart is on the side of the angels. Not only can he make the world go away with a look, but he doesn't ask unnecessary questions. Which doesn't mean I'm not going to have to tell him everything. I am. I will. But not yet.

Right now, I'm a lot more interested in his story. The man is clearly a genius architect, so what the heck is he doing running a department store—stores?

And if those clothes upstairs in the creepy

*bedroom belong to his cousin, the one who com-
missioned this apartment, where is he?*

'Can I help?'

Nat, emptying the trolley, turned at the rare sound of
another human voice in his kitchen. Lucy was standing in
the doorway, a discordant slash of garish green against the
cool grey of the slate and marble surfaces of the kitchen.

A discordant note in his life, knocking him off balance,
sending a fizz of expectancy racing through his veins.

'Shall I put these away?' She didn't wait for an answer,
but picked up a bag of salad leaves and, as she turned, he
saw that she'd taken off the felt boots and striped tights,
that the tunic barely covered her satin-skinned thighs and
that her toenails were painted a bright candy-red that would
have all the boy elves' heads in a spin. Not to mention the
CEO of this department store.

She opened one of the doors to the stainless steel fridge
and he saw her pause for a heartbeat as she realised that,
apart from bottled water, it was empty.

'You don't do a lot of entertaining, do you?'

'I usually eat in one of the store restaurants,' he said.
'It keeps the staff on their toes, knowing I might drop in
at any time.'

'Right.'

'There are eight of them to choose from,' he said, needing to prove that he wasn't totally sad. 'Everything from
Italian to Japanese.'

'Sushi for breakfast?' She didn't wait for an answer.
'The store doesn't open until ten, does it? I don't know
about you, but I'd be gnawing my fingers off by then.'

'It's just as well I ignored your demands to put the porridge back on the shelf, then.' He took one of her hands,

rubbed a thumb over the back of her slender fingers, perfect nails. 'It would be a pity to spoil these.'

'Nathaniel…' The word came out as a gasp.

'Fortunately, the staff canteen opens at seven,' he said, cutting off the little thank you speech he could see she was working up to, letting go of her hand. He didn't want her thanks. He didn't know what he wanted. Or maybe he did. He just wasn't prepared to let go of the past. Admit it. 'It takes time to get everything pitch perfect for the public.'

'Well, that makes sense, I suppose.' She sounded doubtful. 'If you don't like to cook.' She turned back to the island, continued putting away the cold food. 'What are you planning to do for Christmas? I don't imagine the store is open on Christmas Day.'

'No. Obviously, I've tried to persuade the staff that it's a good idea, purely for my own convenience, you understand, but for some reason they won't wear it.'

Bad choice of words.

She wasn't wearing nearly enough. If she was going to stay it was essential that she cover those shapely legs. Those sweet little toes with their shiny red nails. Or he wouldn't be answerable.

Nathaniel frowned and Lucy swallowed. Hard. She was totally losing it.

'I'm sorry. That was unbelievably rude of me. You've probably noticed, but I tend to say the first thing that comes into my head. Obviously, you've got family, friends.'

A cousin, at least.

'I'm never short of invitations,' he agreed, 'but, by the time the big day arrives, all I want to do is open a tin of soup.'

'You can have too much of a good thing, huh?'

'Remind me again,' he invited, 'what exactly is good about it?'

'You don't like Christmas?'

'I repeat, what's good about it?'

'Lots of things. The fun of choosing gifts for the people you love.' No response. He didn't love anyone? No... 'Planning the food?' she offered quickly, not wanting to think about the red rose in the room upstairs. 'Oh, no. You don't cook. How about a brass band playing Christmas carols in the open air? The sense of anticipation. The faces of little children.' She didn't appear to be making much impression with the things that she loved about Christmas so she tried a different tack. 'How about the profits, Nathaniel? Remind me, how much does it cost to take a sleigh ride to Santa's grotto?'

If she'd hoped to provoke him into a show of emotion, she would have been disappointed.

'Would you care to see a breakdown of the costs involved in designing and creating a visual effects spectacular that will satisfy children who've been brought up on CGI?' he enquired, clearly not in the least bit excited by the cost or the finished product. 'You're right, Lucy. Christmas is a rip-off. A tacky piece of commercialism and if I could cancel it I would.'

'I didn't say that!'

'No? Forgive me, but I thought you just did.'

'What I was doing was offering you a personal reason to enjoy it.'

'The profit motive? Sorry, you're going to have to try harder than that.'

'Okay. Come down to the grotto and listen to the little ones for whom it's all still magic, the wonder still shiny-bright.'

'At a price.'

'I know. And I wish every child had the chance to see it.' She reached up for an egg basket, hanging over the island. 'Actually, I wouldn't mind seeing it myself.' Then, because he was a cynic and she was a fool, 'Should any of them ask you, by the way, the reindeer are parked on the roof.'

'They are?'

'Well, obviously. Santa's here so where else would they be?'

'Good point.'

'And you might warn Groceries that there's likely to be a rush on chilli-flavoured cashew nuts. You wouldn't want to miss a sale.'

'That would be tragic.' Nat felt the tension ease from his jaw as his mouth hitched up in the makings of a smile. 'I know I'm going to hate myself for asking this, but why would there be a rush on chilli-flavoured cashew nuts?'

Lucy responded with a careless shrug and he found himself holding his breath, wondering what was coming next.

'I happened to let it slip that Rudolph eats them to keep his nose bright. Dido promised to keep it secret but I can't guarantee that she won't try a little one-upmanship on her sister.'

'What an interesting day you've had, Lucy Bright.'

'It's had its ups and its downs,' she admitted. 'That was definitely an up.'

'Why cashew nuts?'

'Oh, well, peanuts can be a problem. You know. Allergies…' She regarded him steadily, waiting. Then, 'Come on, Nathaniel Hart. Get with the plot.'

Realising he'd missed something, he lifted his brows, inviting her to provide the punchline.

'Elf and safety?'

It took a moment but then he shook his head. 'I do not believe you just said that, Lucy Bright.'

'Actually, neither do I,' she said solemnly. And then she snorted with laughter.

The sound rippled around the kitchen, bouncing off doors, windows, an array of steel tools hanging from the four-sided rail above the island.

Waking everything up, Nat thought, setting up a hum that seemed to vibrate through him until he was laughing, too.

'Do you have a kettle, do you know?' she asked once she'd recovered. Then, as he reached for it, 'I don't need to be waited on.'

'I do know how to boil a kettle. Tea?' he offered. 'Or would you prefer coffee?'

'Oh, tea, I think. Camomile, if you've got it. It's a bit late for coffee.'

Only if you were able to sleep.

She transferred the eggs from the carton to the basket while he filled the kettle, switched it on. Stretched up on her toes to replace it.

Her hair had dried into a froth of little tendrils that curled around her face, against her neck. All she needed were wings and a white dress and she'd look more at home on the top of a Christmas tree than dressed as an elf.

Eggs safe, she picked up a punnet of baby plum tomatoes and looked at them for a moment, then at the plain white china mugs he'd taken from the cupboard, a tiny frown buckling her forehead.

She wasn't beautiful, there was nothing classic about her features, yet there was a sparkle in her green eyes that made everything right. Made something inside him begin to bubble, catch like a motor that hadn't been used in a while, that had to be teased into life with a touch, a smile, laughing lips that begged to be kissed.

Like a limb that had gone to sleep, the return to life hurt.

He turned away, almost with relief, as the kettle boiled and reached for one of a row of polished black canisters.

'It's not camomile,' he apologised, extracting a couple of tea bags. He rarely drank tea and discovered that they were disconcertingly beige in this monochrome world. 'I'm afraid Earl Grey is the best I can do.'

'That will be lovely,' she said, joining him. A warm presence at his side.

He dropped the bags into the mugs, poured on boiling water, looked up.

'You've settled in?' he asked, trying to forget about the kiss.

She nodded.

'You've got everything you need? Toothbrush? Toiletries?'

'Yes, thanks. Everything for the guest who forgot to pack her toilet bag,' she assured him. 'Even a bathrobe. I'll replace the toothbrush.'

'No need.'

'I'd have to buy one, anyway.'

'You'll need more than a toothbrush. You'll need some clothes.' And, before she could object, 'A change of underwear, at least.'

'You have a washing machine, I imagine?'

'There was one included in the specification,' he admitted. 'Along with every other modern convenience known to man.'

'Specified by your cousin. The man with the Gothic taste.'

'Gothic?'

'How else would you describe that room upstairs? It's pure Addams family. All it needs is a belfry for the bats.'

'It would spoil the lines. And let in the rain.'

'Heaven forbid.'

He saw the question in her eyes, then the uncharacteristic hesitation as she decided against it.

'Actually, it's all black and white, glass and brushed stainless steel in the store, too, isn't it?' she said, changing tack. 'I hadn't realised before, but of course down there it's a frame for all that colour. It works.'

'Thanks for that. I think,' he said, but it gave him an opportunity to revisit the subject of clothes. 'Actually, I was wondering, in the interests of aesthetics, if I could encourage you to change into something a little less...green.'

'In the interests of aesthetics?' Her exquisitely threaded eyebrows rose in a pair of questioning little arches. 'Is that an architectural get-out-of-your-kit line, Nathaniel Hart?'

'I wasn't suggesting you stripped off here and now.' Although the idea had considerable appeal.

'Are you sure? It sounded rather like it.'

He managed a shrug. 'I was merely pointing out that they're working clothes. If you're planning to keep up the act, continue to hide out in the grotto, you're going to need them fresh and clean in the morning. House rule,' he said.

'Is that right?' For a moment he thought she was truly offended. Then she grinned. 'Well, snap, Mr Pinstriped Suit. Off with your jacket. Off with your tie and cufflinks!'

Grinning back, he said, 'I'll change if you will. Let's go shopping.'

She was still smiling, but she was shaking her head. 'Until I get a proper job, I won't have any money. And I can't take anything from you, Nathaniel.'

Why not? Presumably, she'd allowed Henshawe to dress her. Which answered that question. But didn't help with the problem.

'Be reasonable, Lucy. You can't live in that.'

'It will be a challenge,' she admitted, but there was a steely glint in those green eyes now, and he battled down the frustration of having an entire store full of clothes he would happily give her, aware that this wasn't about him. This was about her. Her need to re-establish her self-esteem. Recover what had been stolen from her.

'You've got a proper job,' he reminded her, 'at least until Christmas. I'll sub you until the end of the week.'

'You're really going to let me work here?'

'Why not? You seem to have nothing better to do and an elf with a close personal relationship with Rudolph is a real find. Besides,' he pointed out, 'you owe Pam.' It wasn't playing fair, but he was prepared to use every trick in the book to keep her safe. Keep her close.

'Pam might have other ideas if she knew the truth,' she reminded him as she opened a carton of milk, poured a little into each mug. 'What is the going rate for an elf?'

He told her.

'Sorry...' she was going to turn him down? '...that's actually not bad, but even so I wouldn't be able to afford your prices.'

'There's a generous staff discount,' he said.

'For temps?'

'I'm a temp, too.' Long-term, until death us do part...

'Are you?' For a moment it was all there in her eyes. The questions that were piling up, but when he didn't answer all she said was, 'I bet you're on a better hourly rate than me.'

She handed him one of the mugs and turned to lean back against the counter to sip at her tea. He could feel the warmth of her body and he wished he'd taken her advice, taken off his jacket so that there was only his shirt sleeve between them.

'I wonder what happened to the real elf?' she said after a moment. 'The one from Garlands.'

'Maybe, given time to think about it, she didn't want to spend December in a windowless basement,' he said, sipping at his own tea and deciding there were more interesting ways of heating up his, her lips. How close had they been to a kiss on the stairs? An inch, two?

'Maybe. Or maybe, when it started to snow, she decided she'd rather go home and make a snowman.'

'Is that what you'd have done, Lucy?'

'Me? Fat chance. Every minute of every day is fully booked. Or it was. This afternoon I had a meeting with a wedding designer to explore ideas for my fantasy wedding.'

'It may still happen,' he said, glancing down at her, the words like ashes in his mouth.

'Nope. The word "fantasy" is the clue. It means illusory. A supposition resting on no solid ground.'

He wanted to tell her that he was sorry. But it would be a lie and actually she didn't look that upset. The brightness in her green eyes was not a tear but a flash of anger.

'So what should you be doing this evening? If you weren't here, tearing my life's work to shreds.'

'Now?' She pulled a face. 'I should be gussied up in full princess mode for a gala dinner at the Ritz, to celebrate the unveiling today of Lucy B.'

'With you as the star? Well, obviously, that would have been no fun,' he teased.

'Not nearly as much as you'd think. Speeches, smug PR men and endless photographs,' she said. 'Being an elf beats it into a cocked hat.'

'So you're saying that your day hasn't been a total write-off?'

'No,' she said, looking right at him. 'Hand on my heart, I'd have to say that my day hasn't been a total write-off.'

Any other woman and he'd have said she was putting a brave face on it, but something in her expression suggested that she was in earnest.

'Shame about the snowman, though,' she said, turning away as if afraid she'd revealed more of herself than she'd intended. She abandoned her mug. 'It doesn't often snow in London, not like this. I hope the missing elf did seize the day and go out to play.'

'It's not too late.'

'Too late for what?'

'To go out to play.' And where the hell had that come from? 'Build a snowman of your own.'

'Nathaniel!' she protested, but she was laughing and her eyes, which he'd seen filled with fear, mistrust, uncertainty, were now looking out at the falling snow with a childlike yearning and, crazy as it was, he knew he'd said the right thing. And, as if to prove it, she put a hand behind her head, a hand on her hip, arched a brow and, with a wiggle that did his blood pressure no good, said, 'Great idea, honey, but I haven't got a thing to wear.'

'Honey,' he replied, arching right back at her. 'You seem to be forgetting that I'm your fairy godmother.'

Before he could think about what he was going to do, he caught her hand and raced up the stairs with her.

The emptiness hit him as he opened the door, bringing him to an abrupt halt. Lucy was right. This wasn't a bedroom, it was a mausoleum. And that hideous rose...

'Nathaniel...' Her voice was soft behind him, filling the room with life, banishing the shadows. Her warm fingers tightened on his as if she understood. 'It doesn't matter. Leave it.'

'No. Seize the day,' he said, flinging open the door to

the dressing room with its huge walk-in wardrobe filled with plastic-covered ghosts. The colours muted. No scent. Nothing.

He pulled off covers, seeking out warm clothes. Trousers. He pulled half a dozen pairs from hangers. A thick padded jacket. Opened drawers, hunting out shirts, socks. Sweaters. Something thick, warm...

As his hand came down on thistledown wool, it seemed to release a scent that had once been as familiar as the air he breathed and, for a moment, he froze.

Carpe diem.

The words mocked him.

When had he ever seized the day? Just gone for it without a thought for the consequences; been irresponsible? Selfish? Maybe when he'd been eighteen and told his father that he wasn't interested in running a department store, that he was going to be an architect?

Had it taken all the courage, all the strength he possessed to defy, disappoint the man he loved, that he had never been able to summon up the courage to do it again?

'Nathaniel, this is madness,' Lucy called from the bedroom. 'I can't go outside. I don't have any shoes.'

He picked up the sweater, gathered everything else she was likely to need, including a pair of snow boots that he dropped at her feet, doing his best to ignore her wiggling toes with their candy nails.

'They'll be too big,' she protested.

'Wear a couple of pairs of socks.' Then, 'What are you waiting for? It'll all have disappeared by morning.'

'Madness,' she said, but she leapt to her feet and gave him an impulsive hug that took his breath away. She didn't notice, was already grinning as she began to tug the tunic over her head, offering him another glimpse of those full, creamy breasts, this time encased in gossamer-fine black lace.

Breathless? He'd thought he was breathless?

'Downstairs in two minutes,' he said, beating a hasty retreat.

CHAPTER EIGHT

LUCY scrambled into a shirt that didn't quite do up across the bust. Trousers that didn't quite meet around the waist, were too long in the leg. It was crazy stupid. But in a totally wonderful way.

She picked up the thistledown sweater, held it to her cheek for a moment, trying to catch a hint of the woman— thinner, taller than her—who'd owned it. What was she to Nathaniel? Where was she?

Nothing. Not even a trace of scent.

Relieved, she pulled it over her head. It was baggy and long enough to cover the gaps. She tucked the trousers into a pair of snow boots that swallowed the excess and the feather-light down-filled coat, the kind you might wear on a skiing holiday, had room enough to spare.

Hat, scarf.

She didn't bother to check her reflection in the mirror. She didn't need confirmation that she looked a mess. Some things it was better not to know. Instead, she picked up the gloves and, leaving behind her a room that no longer looked cold but resembled the aftermath of a jumble sale, she stomped down the stairs in her too-big boots.

By the time she'd re-applied lipstick to protect her lips from the cold, picked up her phone and purse, Nathaniel was impatiently pacing the living room.

'Two minutes, I said!'

About to reiterate that this was madness, the words died on her lips. He'd abandoned the pinstripes for jeans, a jacket similar to the one she was wearing. The focused, controlled businessman had been replaced by a caged tiger scenting escape.

'Yes, boss,' she said cheekily, pulling on her gloves as they used the private lift which took them straight to the underground car park.

He boosted her up into the seat of a black Range Rover, climbed up beside her.

'Better duck down,' he said as they approached the barrier.

'You don't think...?'

'Unlikely, but better safe than sorry.'

The traffic was light; no one with any sense would be out in this weather unless is was absolutely necessary.

'I think you might be optimistic about it thawing by morning,' she said.

'Want to risk leaving it for another day?'

'No way!'

'Thought not.'

Neither of them spoke again until he'd driven through Hyde Park and parked near the Serpentine Bridge.

'Oh, wow,' she said, staring across the utterly still, freezing waters of the lake. The acres of white, disappearing into the thick, whirling snow. 'Just...wow,' again as she unclipped the seat belt, opened the door, letting in a flurry of snow.

She didn't stop to think, but slid down, spun around in it, grinning as Nathaniel caught her hand and they ran across the blank canvas, leaving their footprints in the snow.

She picked up a handful and flung a snowball at him,

yelling as he retaliated, scoring a hit as snow found its way inside her jacket.

Lucy was right, Nat thought as they gathered snow, piling it up, laughing like a couple of kids. This was crazy. But in the best possible way. A little bit of magic that, like the kids visiting the grotto, was making a memory that would stay with him.

They rolled a giant snowball into a body, piling up more snow around its base before adding a head.

Drivers, making their way through the park, hooted encouragement but, as Lucy waved back, he caught her hand, afraid that someone might decide to stop and crash their snowman party.

He wasn't afraid that she'd be recognized. They were far enough from the street lights and the snow blurred everything. It was just that, selfishly, he didn't want to share it, share her, with anyone.

She looked up, eyes shining, snowflakes sticking to her lashes, the curls sticking out from beneath her hat, clinging for a moment to her lips before melting against their warmth.

'Are we done?' he said before he completely lost it and did in reality what he'd imagined in his head a dozen times: kiss her senseless. Or maybe that was him. The one without any sense. 'Is it big enough?'

'Not it. She. Lily.'

'A girl snowman?'

She added two handfuls of snow, patting it into shape, giving her curves.

'She is now.' She grinned up at him. 'Equal opportunities for all. Fairy godmothers. Santas. Snowmen. I wish we'd brought some dressing up clothes for her.'

He removed the pull-on fleece hat he was wearing and tucked it onto Lily's head.

'Oh, cute,' she said and draped the scarf she was wearing around her like a stole. Then she took her phone from her pocket and took a picture.

'Give it to me. I'll take a picture of both of you.'

She crouched down, her arm around the snow lady, and gave him a hundred watt smile. Then she said, 'No, wait, you should be in it, too. A reminder of how much trouble you can get into when you catch a stranger on the stairs.'

'You think?' he said, folding himself up beside her, holding the phone at arm's length. 'Closer,' he said, putting his arm around her, pulling her close so that her cheek was pressed against his and he could feel her giggling.

'We must look like a couple of Michelin men.'

'Speak for yourself,' he said, turning to look at her. Her eyes were shining, lit up, her mouth just inches from his own in a rerun of that moment on the stairs when the world went away.

Had it ever come back?

He fired off the flash before he forgot all his good intentions.

'How's that?' he said, showing her.

'Perfect,' she said, looking over his arm. 'Can I send them to my diary?'

'As a reminder of a crazy moment in the snow?'

'As a reminder that not all men are mendacious rats,' she said. 'That once in a while Prince Charming is the real deal.'

'No...' Not him. Wrong fairy tale. He was the Beast, woken by Beauty from a long darkness of the soul.

But she had fallen back in the snow, laughing as she swept her arms up and down to make a snow angel.

'Come on. You too,' she urged, laughing, and he joined in, sweeping his arms up and down until their gloved hands met. He looked across at her, lying in the snow, golden curls peeping out from beneath her hat, laughing as the huge flakes settled over her face, licking them from her lips.

'What do they taste of?' he asked.

She didn't hesitate. 'Happiness.' And then she looked at him. 'Want to share?'

She didn't wait for his answer, but rolled over so that her body bumped into his, her face above him.

There were moments—rare moments, perfect moments—when the world seemed to pause on its axis, giving you an extra heartbeat of time.

It had happened when he'd caught her on the stairs and, as her laughing lips touched his, a simple gift, and cold, wet, minty-sweet happiness seeped through him, warming him with her passionate grasp on life, it happened again, more, much more than any imagined kiss.

The world stood still and he seized the moment, lifting his hands to cradle her head, slanting his mouth against hers as the warmth became an inferno hot enough to touch the permafrost that had invaded his soul.

Her kitten eyes were more gold than green as she raised her lids. Then touched her lips to his cheek, tasted them with her tongue.

'One of us is crying,' she said.

He rubbed a gloved thumb over her cheek. 'Maybe we both are.'

'With happiness,' she declared.

'Or maybe it's just our eyes watering with the cold. I need to stand up before my butt freezes to the ground.' And, before he could change his mind, he lifted her aside, stood up.

'I've messed up your snow angel,' she said as he reached out a hand to help her to her feet.

'That's okay. I'm no angel,' he said.

'Who is?'

'If I had a Christmas tree, I'd put you on top of it,' he said and, beyond helping himself, he touched his knuckles to her cheek, kissed her again. Just a touch, but somehow more intense for its sweetness. A promise... 'Do you want a picture of your angel?' he asked, forcing himself to take a step back.

'Please.' Then, as if she, too, needed to distract herself from the intensity of the moment, 'I don't suppose you have such a thing as a piece of paper?'

He searched through his pockets, found an envelope. 'Will this do?'

'Perfect.' And, using a lipstick, she wrote in big block capitals: LUCYB WOZ HERE!

She propped it on the front of the snow lady, put out her hand for the phone and took a snap.

'Great. Tweet time, I think,' she said, pulling off her glove with her teeth and, struggling with cold fingers, keyed in a message.

Thanks for the good vibes, tweeps. Here's a tweetpic, just to let you know that I'm safe. #findLucyB LucyB, Wed 1 Dec 22:43

Lucy lifted the phone, looking over her shoulder at him. 'What do you think? Will that have them all running around in the snow?'

'Is that the plan?' he asked as she pressed 'send'.

'I don't have a plan,' she said, lifting her hand to his cheek, pressing her lips against it. Then, as she looked up at him the smile died, 'Thank you, Nathaniel.'

'I should be thanking you. If it wasn't for you, I'd be inside going through the daily sales figures instead of finding my inner child.'

'Inside in the warm,' she said, turning away to give the

snow lady a hug. 'Stay cool, Lily.' Then she looked up. 'It's stopped snowing.'

'I told you. It'll all be gone by tomorrow. Everything will be back to normal.'

'Will it?'

She sounded less than happy at the prospect. Which made two of them.

'We've still got tonight. Are you hungry?'

Her eyes lit up. 'Absolutely starving.'

Diary update: *Fun and frolics in the park with Nathaniel. I didn't see that coming and neither, I suspect, did he. I have to admit that making a snowman—snow lady—in the park at ten o'clock at night in a blizzard is probably not the most sensible thing I've ever done. And it's getting hard to top the stupid ones I've done today.*

And then he kissed me. No, wait, I kissed him. We kissed each other. Lying in the snow.

'I know what this is all about, you know.' Lucy gave him a sideways grin as they stood on the Embankment overlooking the river, tucking into hot dogs. 'Why we're having hot dogs. You just don't want all that nasty bright yellow eggy, cheesy stuff in your kitchen.'

'It's not that.'

Nat took out his phone and snapped her as she sucked a piece of onion into her mouth.

'Hey, not fair!'

'One more for your fans,' he said, lifting it out of reach as she made a grab for it. 'The truth of the matter, Lucy B, is that I couldn't make an omelette to save my life.'

For some reason she seemed to think that was funny.

They'd laughed a lot.

She'd laughed at a couple of outrageous Santa incidents he'd shared from way back in the history of the store. He'd laughed at her stories about a day-care nursery where she'd worked. It was obvious how much she loved the children she'd worked with. From a momentary wistfulness in her look, how much she missed them.

As she'd talked, laughed, all the strain had seeped out of her limbs and her face and she'd told him enough about her character—far more than she realised—to reassure him that she was on the level.

'Actually, this is great. Crazy perfect.' She bumped shoulders with him. 'Thank you.'

'My pleasure,' he said, wrapping his arm around her waist, wanting to keep her close. And it was. Golden curls peeped out from beneath her hat, framing a face lit up, almost translucent in the lamplight.

And, as the strain had eased from her face, the knots deep in his own belly had begun to unravel, at least until that second kiss. At which point they had been replaced by a different kind of tension.

'I hope the missing elf had as much fun as we have,' she said. 'I owe her a lot.'

'Me too,' he said. 'I'll check with HR first thing to see if there were any messages. Deflect any problems.'

'Why?' she asked, her tongue curling out to catch an errant onion. 'Why would you do that? Any of this?'

Good question.

She looked up. 'What happened, Nathaniel? On the stairs.'

Another good question.

'I don't know,' he admitted. That something had happened—something momentous—was beyond doubt. 'I can tell you why I noticed you.'

'That's a start.'

'It was your hair… The way it seemed to float around your head like a halo. It reminded me of someone.'

Quite suddenly, Lucy lost her appetite. What had she expected him to say? That he'd been captivated at a glance. Lie to her? She'd had enough lies to last her a lifetime.

'The woman these clothes belong to?' she asked, pushing it.

'Claudia. Her name was Claudia. She was my cousin's wife.'

'You were in love with her?' Stupid question. Of course he was.

'We both were. I met her at university, dated her, but when I brought her home she met Christopher and after that it was always him. It didn't stop Chris obsessing that we were having an affair when we worked together on the store design.'

She lifted her hand to the bruise at her temple, gently rubbing her fingers over the sore spot, remembering his concern.

'He was abusive,' she said.

'I believe so. She used to brush aside any concern, say she bruised at a touch. Was always walking into things. Maybe she was. She wasn't eating properly, fighting an addiction to tranquillisers. Then one day I caught her running, terrified. I held her,' he said. 'Just held her, begged her to leave him. Not for me. For herself. And then Chris caught up with her, held out his hand to her and, without a word, she took it. Walked away with him. It was as if she had no will.' He glanced at her. 'It was just the hair, Lucy. You're not a bit like her.'

'No,' she said. 'I'm shorter, fatter…' He frowned and she rushed on, 'You're talking about her in the past tense.'

'There was an accident. Chris always drove too fast, even though he knew it terrified her. Probably *because* it terrified her. It's all about control, isn't it?' He looked away for a moment, but then looked back. 'She died instantly. He's in a wheelchair, paralysed from the neck down.'

She shivered, but not with the cold, and he turned to her, put his arms around her. Held her. Just as he'd held Claudia, she thought and, much as she wanted to stay there, in his arms, she pulled away.

'I have no reason to protect Rupert Henshawe, Nathaniel. He does not control me.'

'Doesn't he?' He shook his head, as if he knew the answer. 'Reason has nothing to do with it,' he said. Then, before she could deny it, 'It was my fault. I should never have come back. Never accepted the commission.'

'Why did you?'

'Family. Guilt. I turned my back on family tradition and it broke my father's heart. It was a way to make up for that.'

'And, after the accident, you stepped in to look after things?'

'There was no one else.'

'No one else called Hart, maybe. Is Christopher punishing you for what happened to him?' she asked. 'Or are you punishing yourself for not saving Claudia?' He didn't answer. Maybe he didn't know the answer. 'Who is it who leaves the rose, Nathaniel?'

'That's enough, Lucy,' he said sharply.

'It's him, isn't it? A daily reminder that she loved him. He can't abuse his wife any more, frighten her, hurt her, because she's beyond his reach,' she continued, recklessly ignoring the warning. 'So he's abusing you instead.'

There was a long moment of silence.

So not bright, Lucy Bright.

Blown it, Lucy Bright.

And then he touched her cheek with his cold hand. A gesture that said a hundred times more than words.

'Bright by name, bright by nature. Good guess, but you're not entirely right. I'm punishing myself for failing to protect her. But I'm punishing him, too. Even while it gives him pleasure to know that I've been jerked back into the family business, robbed of something I loved, at the same time it's eating him alive to know that I'm in control. In his place.'

'He had Claudia.'

'Yes, he had Claudia. His tragedy, and ultimately hers, is that he never believed that she could love him more than me. That he always thought of himself as second choice in all things.'

'Let it go, Nathaniel. If you don't, it will destroy you and then he'll have killed you both.'

'I know,' he said, looking at her. 'I know.' And somehow she was the one holding him. Hugging him to her, holding him safe. She could have stayed there for ever, making their own warm, safe space in an icy world. Then he dropped a kiss on the top of her head. 'Your turn, Lucy.'

'Mine?' She looked up at him.

'That was the deal. I tell you mine and you tell me yours. Tell me what happened on the stairs.'

'I...' About to deny it, she thought better of it. 'I don't know. I was in a bit of a state, confused. An emotional basket case.'

'That would explain it,' he replied dryly, 'but I have to tell you that, between your criticism of the penthouse and the basket case explanation of a stop-the-world-moment, you are not doing a lot for my ego.'

'I didn't mean...'

Lucy faltered. She didn't know what she meant. She was more confused now than she had been then. When he'd caught her, their eyes had met and the instant connection had entirely bypassed her brain.

Her response to him had been entirely physical, without thought or reason. Completely honest. Without guile. Innocent.

'I wanted you to kiss me,' she said. Then, because being honest really mattered, 'I wanted you.'

Even in the light from the street lamps, Nat could see the blush heat Lucy's cheeks. Felt an answering and equally primitive rush, a desire to recapture that atavistic moment of connection. The caveman response, with no need for words or complicated ritual.

Her honesty shamed him. He'd wanted her, too, with a raw urgency that shocked the civilised man. It was the same primal instinct that urged him to protect her. They were two sides of the same basic need for survival. Take the woman, plant your seed and then protect her against the world because she was your future. And he would. From what, he wasn't entirely certain, only that this time he wouldn't stand back. Wouldn't fail. No matter what the cost.

The 'no involvement' mantra had gone right out of the window the moment he'd suggested this mad adventure.

That first life-changing encounter had given him back something of himself. The kisses they'd shared in the snow had broken through a barrier. More would have them naked, in bed. That was why he'd stopped by the hot dog stall instead of taking her straight home.

'"I wanted you",' he repeated thoughtfully. 'Maybe it could do with a little work. I was thinking that it was one of those perfect, never to be repeated, once-in-a-lifetime moments when everything seems to drop into place.'

She pulled a wry smile. 'You'd think so, wouldn't you. But they will keep happening to me.'

'You're telling me that you keep meeting strangers you want to kiss?' he asked, his voice even, but the caveman response was, he discovered, a lot more powerful than the civilised veneer would suggest.

'Oh, not *kiss*.' Her smile deepened. 'That was a bonus feature. And of course last time it wasn't a chance encounter, but stage-managed, so actually you're right. Once-in-a-lifetime it is.'

'Stage-managed?'

'You want the story.' She nodded as if she'd been expecting that. 'I warn you that it's long. You'll probably want another hot dog. Extra onions for me.'

He returned with two fresh hot dogs, dripping with mustard and onions, and leaned back against the wall, his shoulder just touching hers. Just so that she'd know he was there.

Giving her courage to tell her story. Face the betrayal head-on.

'The Henshawe Corporation's High Street fashion chain had lost market share,' she began. 'It was no longer hot so they made the decision to give the stores a new look, a new name. Re-brand it. Take it upmarket.'

Lucy bit into the bun, chewed it for a while, watching a police launch moving slowly up the river, the lights dancing on the water, while she gathered her thoughts.

Nathaniel slipped his arm around her shoulder as if it was the most natural thing in the world.

'They went to their PR company, as you do,' she said, 'and commissioned them to come up with a strategy to launch the new brand. One that would not only garner maximum media coverage, but engage their target consumer audience of young women who read gossip magazines and aspire to be the wife, or at least the girlfriend, of a top sports star.'

'Or, failing that, one of the minor royals,' he said, raising a smile.

'You've got it.'

'So far, so standard.'

'Their first step was to set up focus groups to find out what that group were looking for. Get feedback on likely "names" to launch the new brand.'

'Classy, stylish, sexy clothes. Good value. A label with cachet. You don't need a focus group to tell you that,' he said.

'No, but they were surprised to discover that concerns were raised about sweatshop labour. And then someone said wouldn't it be great if they used an ordinary girl, someone like them, rather than a celebrity to be the face of the store.'

'What they meant was one of them.'

'Undoubtedly,' she said. 'But it gave the PR firm their hook. Their media campaign. All they needed was an ordinary girl.'

'So how did they find you, Miss Ordinary?' he asked.

'They advertised for a junior clerical assistant.'

'Interesting approach,' he said dryly. 'You ticked all the boxes?'

'Good grief, no. I wasn't thin enough, tall enough, pretty enough or even smart enough.'

It was all there in the file. Painful reading.

'I thought they wanted ordinary.'

'Ordinary in quotes,' she said, using her fingers to make little quote marks.

'You must have had something.'

'Thanks for that,' she said, waving towards the road, where the cars were moving slowly past in the slushy conditions.

'Who are you waving to?'

'My ego and yours, hand in hand, hitching a ride out of here,' she said, her breath smoking away in the cold air. Her mouth tilting up in a grin. Because, honestly, standing here with Nathaniel, it did all seem very petty. Very small stuff. Except, of course, it wasn't that simple.

'Actually, I happen to think you're pretty special,' he said, capturing her hand, wrapping it in his. 'But we both know that you're not classic model material.'

'You're right. I know it, you know it, the world knows it. But I had three things going for me.' They'd handily itemised them on a memo. 'First, I had a story. Abandoned as a baby—'

'Abandoned?'

'The classic baby in a cardboard box story, me.'

He made no comment. Well, what could anyone say?

'I had a dozen foster homes,' she continued, 'a fractured education that left me unqualified to do anything other than take care of other people's children. Not that I was qualified for that, but it was something I'd been doing since I was a kid myself.'

'You truly were Cinderella,' he said, getting it.

'I truly was,' she confirmed.

The hot dog was gone and she reached for her coffee. Took a sip. It was hot.

'Second?' he prompted.

'I had ambition. I worked in a day-care nursery from eight-thirty until six, then evenings as a waitress to put myself through night school to get a diploma in business studies.'

'Cinderella, but not one sitting around waiting for her fairy godmother to come along with her magic wand.'

He was quick.

'Cinderella doing it for herself,' she confirmed. 'Not that

it did me much good. I didn't get a single interview until I applied for the Henshawe job.'

'It's tough out there.'

'Tell me about it. I really, really needed that job and when they asked me why I wanted to work for the company I didn't hold back. I let them have it with both barrels. The whole determination to make something of my life speech. Oscar-winning stuff, Nathaniel. They actually applauded.'

'They were from the PR company, I take it?'

'How did you guess?'

'HR managers tend to be a little less impressionable. You said you had three things.'

'My third lucky break was that some woman on the team was bright enough to realise that I was exactly the kind of woman who would be walking in off the street, desperate for something to make her look fabulous. Let's face it, if the gold-standard was a size-zero, six-foot supermodel, the reflection in the dressing room mirror was always going to be a disappointment.'

'But if they compared themselves with you... Who is this PR company? I could use that kind of out of the box thinking.'

'Oh, I don't deny they're good.'

'Sorry. Your story. So, having applauded your audition, they told you what the part would be?'

'No.'

'No?'

'You're missing the point. I was going to be a genuine "ordinary" girl who had been picked from among his staff. I had to believe in the story before I could sell it.'

'Did I say they were good?'

'Oh, there's more. Someone added a note on the bottom of their report to the effect that this was going to be a real fairy tale. And then they started thinking so far out of the box they were on another planet.'

His hand tightened on hers. 'It was all a set-up? Not just the job, the discovery...'

'I had a phone call the day after my interview, offering me the job. I started the following week and I have to tell you that it was the most boring week of my life. I was climbing the walls by Friday afternoon, wondering how long I could stand it. Then I was sent up to the top floor with a pile of files, got knocked off my feet by a speeding executive and there was Rupert Henshawe, perfectly placed to pick me up, sit me in his office, give me coffee from his personal coffee-maker while his chauffeur was summoned to take me home. And, while we waited, he asked me about my job, whether I liked working for the company. I'd heard he was as hard as nails. Terrifying if you made a mistake. But he was so kind. Utterly...' she shrugged '...charming.'

'I'd heard he was a smooth operator.'

'I had flowers and a note on Saturday. Lunch in the country on Sunday. Picture in the tabloids on Monday.'

CHAPTER NINE

'ARE you telling me that you didn't have a clue?'

'Not until today,' she admitted. 'Dumb or what?'

'Don't be so hard on yourself. You saw what he wanted you to see.'

'What I wanted to believe. Until today. I was late and, since I didn't have time to go home and pick up my copy of the wedding file, I decided to borrow the one in Rupert's office. That's when I stumbled across the one labelled "The Cinderella Project".'

She still remembered the little prickle at the base of her neck when she'd seen it.

'But the romance, the engagement?'

She understood what he was asking. 'There is no sex in fairy tales, Nathaniel. My Prince Charming okayed the plan, but only with the proviso...' written in his own hand '...that he didn't have to "sleep with the girl".' More of those quote marks.

'So he's gay?'

She blinked. 'Why would you say that?'

He shook his head. 'Just thinking out loud.'

She stared at him for a moment. Was he saying what she thought he was saying? That the only reason a man wouldn't want to sleep with her was because...?

'No...'

He responded with a lift of those expressive eyebrows. 'You'd have thought someone so good at the details would have made a little more effort. That's all I'm saying.'

'Yes... No...' She blushed. 'I wasn't exactly throwing myself at him.'

'No? How come I got so lucky?' She dug him in the ribs with her elbow. In response, he put his arm around her. 'You throw, I'll catch,' he said and, without stopping to think, she stood on tiptoe and put her arms around his neck. He didn't let her down, scooping her up so that she was off the ground, grinning as he spun her around, kissing her before he set her back on her feet.

'Thanks,' she said.

'Entirely my pleasure,' he assured her, still holding her close. 'But I don't understand. If there was no great romance, no passion, why did you accept his proposal, Lucy?'

'Because I bought the fairy story.'

She was still buying it, she thought, glancing up at Nathaniel. She really needed to get a grip on reality.

'The breakup scenario is already written, by the way,' she said, before he could say anything. Pulling away. 'Apparently, I'm going to call the wedding off because Rupert is a workaholic, too absorbed in business to spend time with me. True, as it happens. Sadness, but no recriminations. Nothing sordid. Just a quiet fade out of the relationship once the stores are open and the brand established.'

'You went seriously off message this afternoon.'

'I lost the plot big time, but that's what you get for employing amateurs.'

'I can see why he's desperate to get the file back. The tabloids would have a field day with this.' And, from looking deep into her eyes, he was suddenly looking at something in the distance above her head. 'I'm not just talking about his underactive libido.' She didn't miss the edge to his voice as he added, 'You could make a fortune.'

'Yes, I could. I could have phoned one of the tabloids this afternoon. But I don't want a drama, Nathaniel. I just want to disappear. Get my life back. Be ordinary.'

'But you're Lucy B,' he pointed out.

'I know. That's why I can't let him get away with what he's doing. Why I can't just disappear. Because that's not the end of it.'

'There's more?'

'He wants his file back because all that lovely stuff about fair trade fashion is a bunch of baloney.'

'Baloney?'

'Lies, falsehoods, untruths. There is a fair trade company, but it's just a front. The actual clothes, shoes, accessories will still be made by the same sweatshop workers he used for the old stuff. That's why he's desperate to retrieve the file.'

He said just one word. Then, 'I'm sorry...'

'No need to apologise. You've got it. The man has all the morals of a cowpat.' She stuffed her hands deep in her pockets. 'That's why I was so angry. Why I couldn't think straight. When the media circus took off like a rocket, bigger than anything they had imagined, and a headline writer shortened my name to Lucy B, Marketing ditched the names they'd been playing with and grabbed it. He's going to use my name—on the shop fronts, on the labels, everywhere—use me to sell his lie. That's what today's press conference was about. To unveil the look of the stores. Tell the world about the jobs he's creating, both here and in the Third World. Impress the public with his new caring image, impress the shareholders with profit forecasts.'

'That's...' For a moment he didn't seem to be able to find a word. And then he did. 'Dangerous.'

Not reassuring—she'd been a lot less bothered by the expletive—and, despite the down jacket, she shivered.

'You're cold,' he said. 'Let's go home. Get you back in the warm.'

Diary update: *I have to admit that when Nathaniel asked me if I was hungry I didn't anticipate a hot dog from a stall on the Strand, but it was junk food at its finest. And the onions were piled up high enough to bring tears of joy to the eyes of the government's diet Tsar. But then it's been that sort of day. Surprises all round. Horrible ones, delicious ones and a man a girl could love. Not fairy tale falling in love, but the genuine article.*

Will everything be back to normal tomorrow?

Can anything ever be normal again?

What is normal?

Nathaniel didn't say anything until they were near the store, then he reached out and, hand on her arm, said, 'Out of sight, I think.'

She didn't argue, but ducked down until the barrier clanged behind them and he'd pulled into a parking bay and switched off the engine. Released his seat belt.

'You saw something?' she asked as she slid down from the seat without waiting for him to help her.

Nat shook his head, put his arm around her shoulders and swept her towards the lift, wanting her inside, out of sight. Regretting the crazy impulse to go out in the snow. Anyone might have seen her.

The guy at the hot dog stall wouldn't forget two idiots who'd gone out to play in the snow, stood for ever, eating hot dogs and talking.

'What's bothering you?' she asked.

'I hadn't realised… This is a lot more serious than I thought, Lucy.'

He keyed in the code and breathed more easily when the door clicked shut behind them, shedding his coat and gloves, kicking off his boots. It was probably the first time he'd actually been glad to be home since he'd moved into the apartment. The first time it had felt like home. A sanctuary.

'You're scaring me,' Lucy said, cold hands fumbling with her zip.

He stopped her. Not cold, just shaking, he discovered and, instead of unzipping it for her, he put his arms around her, held her, because he was scared for her.

This wasn't simply some romance gone wrong. It wasn't even just an amoral PR campaign that meant heads would roll right up to boardroom level.

'Nathaniel? Now you're really worrying me!'

He let her go, unzipped her jacket, helped her out of it.

'Okay. While the fake romance would be an embarrassment to Henshawe, I've no doubt he could contain the damage, but the fair trade thing is fraud.'

'Fraud?'

'It's going to seriously damage him and the Henshawe Corporation when it gets out. The Lucy B chain will be history, his shareholders will want blood and he'll be facing a police investigation.'

'You're talking jail time?' she asked, shocked.

'He's probably shredding papers as fast as he can right now. Talking to his suppliers to cover his tracks. But, while you've got his file, written proof of what he did, he's not safe and I believe that a man who has the morals of a cowpat would go to any lengths to stop that from happening.'

'You're saying that I'm in danger?'

Before he could answer, the phone rang and he unhooked it from the wall. 'Hart.'

'Nat, it's Bryan. Sorry to disturb you, but I've just had a call from the police.'

His heart rate picked up. 'And?'

'It seems they've had a missing person report. A woman called Lucy Bright. The WAG of some billionaire. She was last seen heading this way just after four this afternoon and appears to have vanished off the face of the earth. I wouldn't have bothered you, but the timing is right and the description matches the woman you saw this afternoon.'

'Did you mention that to the police?' he asked, reaching out a hand as he saw the colour drain from Lucy's face.

'No. It might not have been her and I assumed that you wouldn't want policemen crawling all over the store talking to the staff. Or the ensuing press invasion. Not until we're sure, anyway.'

'Good call.'

'I searched the name on the internet and I'm about to send you a photograph as an email attachment. In the meantime, I've initiated a sweep of the premises, just to cover ourselves.'

'Right...' Then, 'You were in the force, Bryan. Isn't it unusual for them to get involved in something like this so quickly?'

'It depends who's missing. And why.'

Nat listened as he detailed all the likely reasons why the police had got involved so quickly. Suspected violence, theft... He never took his eyes off Lucy who, her free hand to her mouth, was watching him with growing apprehension.

'I'll get back to you. In the meantime, keep me posted.'

Lucy was numb. The minute Nathaniel had picked up the phone she'd known something was wrong. And when she'd heard him say the word police she'd known the game was up.

'The police? They've been here? Looking for me?'

'Just a phone call.'

Just!

'You've been reported missing and they're following up on a suggestion that you were last seen entering the store.'

'They're not going to give up, are they? I'm so sorry to have involved you in this, Nathaniel, but I can't believe that Rupert had the nerve to involve the police.'

'You stole a file,' he pointed out. 'One filled with sensitive commercial information.'

'I know, but…' Then, 'Are you saying that he's had the nerve to accuse me of stealing?'

'Not officially.'

'So what?'

'He could be using the fact that there has been a campaign by your fans on the social media sites to put pressure on them. Apparently, the most used hashtag in the last few hours has been #findLucyB.'

'Well, colour me surprised.'

'You're not impressed that you inspire such devotion?'

'Not desperately. I have no doubt that it was instigated by the Henshawe PR team. Why waste time looking for someone when you can persuade half a million people to do it for you? Get a little hysteria going. But I still don't understand. The police don't normally bother about missing persons unless there's blood on the carpet. Do they?' she pressed when he didn't immediately answer.

'Not normally. Not this soon. It must have been the call from your mother that did the trick.'

Lucy froze.

'My mother?'

'She gave an emotional doorstep interview, pleading with anyone who knows where you are to call her. It's probably online if you want to see it.'

'No! I don't. She's not my mother,' she said. 'I told you. I don't have a mother.'

'Lucy—'

'She's a fake,' she said quickly, all the peace, the pleasure of their evening together dissipating in that bitter reality. 'Just another lie dreamed up to keep the press engaged.' The worst one. The cruellest one. The rest she might abhor, but they, at least, had a purpose. 'What's a fairy tale without a wicked witch…?'

Except that she hadn't been wicked. She'd been fifteen. Abandoned by an abusive boyfriend. Alone and afraid.

Lies…

Before she could move, Nathaniel had his arms around her, holding her rigid body, murmuring soft calming sounds that purred through her until she finally stopped shaking. He held her while her silent, angry tears soaked his T-shirt. Held her until the tension seeped from her limbs and she melted against him.

Just held her.

It was a technique she used to calm distraught children, holding them tight so that they'd feel safe even when they fought her—her promise that, whatever they did, she would not let go. And, even as she broke down, buried her face in his shoulder and sobbed like a baby while his hands gently stroked her back, in the dark recesses of her mind, she recognized that this was something he'd done before.

That she shouldn't read more into it than a simple

gesture of comfort and gradually she began to withdraw. Ease away.

She was a survivor. She'd taken everything that life could throw at her and she'd take this, come through it. She lifted her head, straightened her shoulders, putting herself back together, piece by piece, something she'd done times without number.

But never before had the loss of contact felt so personal, the empty space between two bodies quite so cold.

Then, as she brushed her fingers, palms over her cheeks to dry them, Nathaniel took away her hands, tugged up the edge of his T-shirt and used it to very tenderly dab them dry.

'I'm sorry,' she said quickly, pulling away from him before the tears began to fall again. 'I didn't plan to weep all over you.'

His response was a crooked smile and, making a pretence of wringing out his T-shirt between his hands, making a joke of it, he said, 'Is that the worst you've got?'

She felt an answering tug at the corner of her own lips. She was still embarrassed at bawling her eyes out, but somehow it didn't seem to matter so much. Nothing seemed to matter when Nathaniel smiled at her.

And that was dangerous.

Not because he was trying to fool her, but because she was capable of fooling herself. Seeing only what she wanted to see. Hearing only what she wanted to hear.

'You have to call the police, Nathaniel. Tell them I'm here.'

'Do I?' he asked. 'I'm perfectly capable of looking a policeman in the eyes and telling him that you're not in the store.'

'No lies,' she insisted. 'Nobody lies...'

'So long as I do it before the store opens tomorrow, it will be the truth.'

'But it wouldn't be the whole truth and nothing but the truth, would it?'

'You care about that?'

'I've been living a lie for the last six months. This afternoon I lied to Pam...'

'You didn't actually lie to her.'

'I didn't tell her the truth, which is the same thing.' She'd actually congratulated herself on her cleverness, which, considering the way she'd berated Rupert for doing the same thing, was double standards any way you looked at it. 'You've been kind, Nathaniel. Not some fairy tale Prince Charming; you're the real thing. A "parfit gentil knyght". But you have the store to think about, your reputation. This is going to be messy and I don't want you involved.'

'It's odd, Lucy, but that's exactly what I told myself this afternoon when I delegated one of my staff to find you, return your shoe, offer you a pair of tights, whatever else you needed. Leave it to someone else to deal with, I thought. Don't get involved.'

'You did that?' For a moment she felt as if she was bathed in a warm blast, like opening an oven door. 'Well, I guess I will need a pair of tights—'

'I was still saying it when I had Henshawe's bullies evicted from the store,' he continued, taking her face in his hands.

'—and shoes. The boots are great, but—'

'And all the time I was driving Pam home and couldn't think of anything but the fear in your beautiful kitten eyes.' Instinctively, she closed them and felt the butterfly touch of his thumbs brush across her lids. His fingers sliding through her hair as he cradled her head. 'I was telling myself to forget it. Whatever it was. That it wasn't my problem. Don't get involved—'

'But, as to the rest,' she cut in, forcing her eyes open, refusing to succumb to his touch, his voice so soft that it seemed to be lost somewhere deep in his throat.

Forcing herself to take responsibility for what had happened. Step away.

'As to the rest,' she said as her retreat was halted by the bulk of the island unit, 'I'll swallow my pride, borrow some clothes and call that taxi. Go to the nearest police station and tell them the truth.'

It was fraud. A crime…

He'd moved with her, his hands still cradled her head, his train of thought unbroken.

'—don't get involved. Telling myself that by the time I got back you'd be long gone.'

'And in the morning,' she persisted, shutting her ears to temptation, 'you can tell the police that I'm not in the store.'

'And that's not being economical with the truth?'

'Only slightly.'

'The truth, since you're so keen on it, Lucy Bright, is that I was involved from the moment I saw you ahead of me on the stairs. Your hair floating like a halo around your head.'

'Well, that's history…'

She was trapped against the island. His hands were a gentle cradle for her face, his body was warming her from breast to knee, the silver glints in his eyes were molten.

'Now I just look like Harpo Marx…'

Not that she could have moved. Every cell in her body had given up, surrendered and, as his gaze slid down to her lips, it was only the counter at her back that was holding her up.

'Your neck…' His thumb brushed her jaw as his hand stroked her neck in a slow, lazy move that sent a wave of heat rippling down to her toes. 'Did you know that the nape of the neck is considered so erotic that geishas leave it unpainted?'

She managed a small noise, nothing that made any sense because, forget necks, napes or any other part of the anatomy, his voice, so low that only her hormones could hear, was doing it for her.

'The way your dress was slipping from your shoulder—'

'It was just a look,' she said in a last-ditch attempt to hang onto whatever sense she possessed. 'A once-in-a-lifetime, never-to-be-repeated look—'

'What are you prepared to risk on that, Lucy Bright? Truth, dare, kiss, promise…'

Her desperate protestations died as, not waiting for her answer, his eyes never leaving her lips, Nathaniel looked at her with that same intensity, the same liquid silver eyes that had turned her core molten, before slowly lowering his mouth to hers.

She watched in slow motion, knowing that it was going to happen, knowing that all she had to do to stop it was answer him.

Say just one word.

If only she could remember what it was. But her brain was lollygagging around somewhere. Out to lunch. Make that dinner…

She slammed her eyes shut a second before he made contact and her world was reduced to touch. The soft warmth of a barely-there kiss. A tingle as her lips demanded more. A breath—his, not hers. She'd sucked air in and it was stuck there as she waited for the promise.

The warmth became heat.

Her lower lip began to tremble.

Someone moaned and her tongue, too thick for her own mouth, reached for his. Touched his lip. Another moment of this torture and she was going to slither between his arms and melt into a messy puddle on the floor at his feet.

Was this the kiss? The promise? Or was it about the truth?

Right now, it didn't seem to matter much. It might be 'just a kiss' but she wanted it. Wanted it and everything that followed.

'You win,' she murmured against his mouth, her eyes still closed.

'Not entirely,' he replied, his voice more a growl than a purr as his hand abandoned her neck to capture her hip, pull her close, as the kiss became the briefest reality before he took a step back, leaving her hot and hungry for more. 'But you most certainly lost and I'm not going to be a gentleman about it. I'm claiming my forfeit.'

At which point her knees gave up the struggle and buckled beneath her.

Nat caught her as she slithered into his arms. 'Hey,' he said, 'it isn't going to be that bad.'

Her throat was thick and she had to clear it. 'It isn't?'

'What did you think? That I was going to demand your body?'

'Noooo...' Dry and thick with disappointment which if she could hear, so could he...'The police,' she muttered, grabbing for reality. 'We have to call them now.'

'You surrendered, Lucy. I won. Remember? Or shall we try that again?' He mistook her hesitation for reluctance. 'I'm going to call my lawyer,' he said, one arm propping her up, the other retrieving his phone from his jacket pocket.

'He'll call the police, reassure them that you're safe. That you'll be available for an interview, at a time convenient to you, if they want to talk to you.'

'Can you do that?'

'I can do that.'

And he did. Right after he'd caught her behind the knees and carried her through to her bedroom, set her down on the bed and pulled off the boots, taking the three pairs of socks she was wearing with them.

He'd stared at her toes for a moment, then flipped open the phone, got some lawyer out of his bed and told him exactly what he wanted. Not just straightening things out with the police—without revealing her whereabouts—but the retrieval of her belongings from the apartment in the Henshawe house.

'I'm running up a big bill, here,' she said when he'd finished.

'True. You're going to have to work right through until Christmas Eve.'

'That's not work. That's fun.'

He grinned. 'Christmas Eve two thousand and twenty.'

'That big, huh? And if I volunteer to cook Christmas lunch for you?'

'Christmas Eve two thousand and fifty.' And his smile faded. 'Here,' he said, handing her the phone. 'Keep this with you. Post the rest of your photographs. Give Henshawe a sleepless night.'

She would rather give Nathaniel one, she thought, but for once held her tongue, just watching him as he adjusted a dial on the wall and the glass darkened, blotting out the lights, the planes passing overhead.

'I'll find you something to sleep in.'

'I'll manage.'

'No doubt, but I'm not sure my blood pressure can take the strain.'

CHAPTER TEN

Diary update: *Okay, this is the last entry for today. I just peeled off the jeans, which were pretty wet around the knees. The snow had got down my neck, too. I hadn't noticed until Nathaniel left me and suddenly I felt horribly cold, so now I'm dictating this as I lie back in a gorgeously scented bubble bath...*

LUCY paused as she heard a tap on her bedroom door.

'Hello?'

'Room service.'

'I didn't—' she began, but the bathroom door opened a crack—it hadn't occurred to her to lock it—and a glossy Hastings & Hart carrier appeared, dangling from long masculine fingers.

'Pyjamas, slippers and a selection of other female necessities, madam.'

She swallowed. 'Nathaniel...'

'Two thousand and fifty-one,' he said, before any of the things bubbling up from her heart could spill over and embarrass them both.

'Two thousand and fifty-one? They had better be designer necessities,' she replied. Keeping it light, light, light...

'Down to the last button,' he assured her, slipping the handles over the door knob, where it would be safe from accidental spills—the man learned fast—and closing the door. She slid down a little lower in the bath, grinning to herself.

She waited a minute, then clicked 'record' and continued her diary update.

Right, where was I? Oh, thawing out in the bath. It's impossible to describe today, except that I'd be happy to cook Nathaniel Hart's Christmas dinner until the end of time. He is unbelievably special. And, I'm certain, deeply unhappy but tomorrow, as Scarlett O'Hara so famously said, is another day. Maybe it will bring a few answers. To my problems. And to his.

That done, she checked her tweets.

@LucyB Loved the snow lady! One of the London Parks, right? Hyde, Regency, Green? More clues! #findLucyB
jenpb, [+] Wed 1 Dec 23:16

@LucyB Hyde Park. I can just make out the Serpentine Bridge in the background. U okay, sweetie? #findLucyB
WelshWitch, [+] Wed 1 Dec 23:17

She blinked, then quickly keyed in a response, posting the pictures Nathaniel had taken.

@jenpb Hyde Park it is. Here's a pic of a snow angel I made. Tucked up safe, thanx, WW. #findLucyB
LucyB, Wed 1 Dec 23:51

* * *

@WelshWitch Safe & well fed as u can see in this pic.
Who needs dinner at the Ritz? Night tweeps. More
in the morning. #findLucyB
LucyB, Wed 1 Dec 23:54

Lucy climbed out of the bath, wrapped herself in the bathrobe, brushed her teeth, did the whole cleanse, tone, moisturise thing with the stuff provided.

Only when she was done with all that did she allow herself the pleasure of opening the carrier.

The pyjamas were white—obviously—but they were spattered with candy-red hearts and she couldn't wait to scramble into them. Fasten the heart-shaped buttons.

The slippers, fuzzy soft ones that you pushed your feet into, matched them. There was even a wrap that tied with a big red bow.

Further down the bag she found underwear. Yummy, silky, lacy underwear. And, right at the bottom, wrapped in tissue, a pair of shoes. Red suede with peep toes, a saucy bow and very high heels.

Not exactly like the ones she'd been wearing, but she couldn't have chosen anything better for herself and she was wearing a great big grin as, her arms full of wrap and undies and shoes, she opened the door. And, for the second time that day, had a heart-stop moment as she saw Nathaniel, this time stretched out on her bed in a pair of worn-thin joggers, a T-shirt so old that whatever had been written on it had long since faded out, hair damp from the shower, bare feet crossed at the ankle.

Exactly the kind of eye candy that any woman would be delighted to find waiting for her after a delicious soak in a scented bath.

Her pleasure was somewhat dimmed by the fact that he was reading the file she'd carefully hidden in the locker room, although she had to admit that the glossy black cover nicely matched the decor.

'I could have been naked,' she exclaimed. Again.

'A man doesn't get that lucky twice in one day,' he said, looking up, holding her gaze for so long that she forgot all about the file. 'But cute will do to be going on with.'

'The jammies *are* sweet,' she said when her heart had settled back into something like its normal rhythm and she could breathe again. 'I particularly love the red. It exactly matches my toenails.' She wiggled them. 'I had these done this morning. Pam made me remove the colour from my fingernails, but she missed these.'

'I can't think how,' he said, 'but I'm glad she did.' Then, 'Tell me, do you talk to yourself in the bath?'

'I was updating my diary. There was a lot to say.'

'It's been a busy day for Lucy B.'

'Buzz, buzz, buzz… Do you want to hear what I said about you?'

'Probably not.'

She told him anyway. 'I said that you were a great kisser, unbelievably special and deeply unhappy. I seem to have missed your talent with a lock pick.'

'I'm working on the happiness thing,' Nat said, grateful for the distraction of the file. 'And I didn't have to pick the lock. We keep a duplicate set of keys to the lockers. People are always losing them.'

'So? What? You wanted to check my story? See if I was telling the truth?' Her grin was long since history.

'If I'd even suspected that you were lying, Lucy, I'd have read the file in my office. I simply wanted to be sure that you had cast iron proof of Henshawe's guilt.'

'And have I?'

'Yes, fortunately. It's in the focus group section. The part where someone raised the fair trade question. There are detailed notes from the individual tasked to look into it and come up with a plan that would make them look good without compromising profits.'

'But—'

'There were a number of options. Higher prices. Lower margins. Cheaper materials. Or the handy solution that he went for. There's a handwritten note at the bottom over Henshawe's initials. "Option Four. Get on with it."'

Nat held it up for her to see and she sat down heavily on the side of the bed. 'So that's it, then. Lucy B down the pan.'

'Wishing you hadn't opened Pandora's box?' he asked.

'Good grief, no.' She looked down at him. 'You can't think that.'

'But you're not happy,' he said, leaving the question unanswered.

'How can I be? People are going to get hurt. Not Rupert. I don't care if he rots in jail,' she declared fervently and the last shreds of tension, doubt left him. She wasn't going to be seduced by the glamour, the millions. Her only thought was for the people who would be hurt when she brought the company down.

'Tell me about it,' he urged, dropping the folder and stretching out an arm, inviting her to lean back against his shoulder.

'It's always the innocents who pay,' she said, snuggling against him. 'I may have hated working there but hundreds of people—ordinary people—rely on the Henshawe Corporation to feed their families.'

'Right.'

'And it isn't just them. There are the shops. If they're not rebranded, they'll close. Hundreds of women will lose their jobs. I've met some of them and they're all so enthusiastic. So excited...'

She slipped down a little, getting more comfortable, her body heavier against him.

'Even the poor devils in the sweatshops will lose out,' he said, resting his chin on her head.

The scent of the soap she'd used was familiar, but on Lucy it was different, somehow.

'I know. But what choice do I have?' She fought a yawn. 'The man's a liar, a cheat and a crook.'

'List your options,' he suggested. 'One, you go to the police. Bring him and his company down.'

'It's too horrible to think about. Can I go to sleep now?' She closed her eyes.

'Okay. Two, you could sell him out to the tabloids, write a book, make a fortune.'

'Same result, except I get rich.'

'You could share the money amongst the people who lose their jobs.'

'Not rich enough to make a difference to them,' she said, her cheek pressed into his chest.

'No, not rich enough for that. There's option three, the one where you walk away and let him get on with it.'

'Nnngg.'

'No? How about threatening him with exposure? You could force him to clean up his act in return for playing out the role as written? Number four, sticking with the plan, but with you in the driving seat.'

'Wdntrstim,' she mumbled.

'No. Neither would I.' Then, 'What about me, Lucy? Could you trust me?'

No answer.

He didn't need one. She was curled up against him, defenceless as a baby. She'd seen through his guard, peered into his darkest places, knew him as few people did.

And he knew her, too. She lived who she was. Caring for others, even when her own world was crumbling around her.

He was, without question…involved.

And deeply happy to be so.

The engine had caught, the motor was running and the road ahead might have bumps in it but it was leading exactly where he wanted to be.

'Hey, into bed with you,' he said, tearing himself away. He didn't want to leave her, lose the soft warmth of her breast, her thighs curled against him. He wanted, for the first time in as long as he could remember, to lie beside a woman, sleep with her.

Just sleep.

Close his eyes and know she was there. Know she would be the first thing he saw when he woke. Know that he would be the first thing she saw when she opened her green-gold eyes and smile because that one thing made her happy.

But this wasn't about him. He pulled the cover from beneath her and she rolled into the warm space where he'd been lying, her face in the pillow.

'Big day tomorrow.'

'T'day…'

She was right. It was gone midnight. Or did she mean that it had been a big day today? Not just for her.

'Furs day rest life,' she mumbled.

He stood for a moment watching every scrap of tension leave her body as she melted into sleep almost before the jumble of words had left her mouth.

Today was the first day of the rest of her life. Or did she mean his?

He looked around at the room that, just hours before, had been sterile and empty. Clothes dropped where she'd left them. The bright red splash of her coat across the chair. A muddle. Untidy. Just like life.

There were no easy solutions, no perfect answers. You did what you had to do and got on with it. He'd been a successful architect, but he'd been raised to this. With no heart in it, he'd expanded the company out of all recognition. What could he do if he stopped looking back, regretting the life he'd lost and instead looked forward? Seized the day? Seized the life he'd been given?

Time to do a little homework. Arrange a meeting with the H&H trustees.

'Hey, sleepy-head.'

'Nnng…' She pushed her face deeper into the pillow. Today was not going to be fun and she was in no hurry for it to start.

There was a touch to her shoulder and, giving up, she opened her eyes, saw the tempting curl of steam rising from a bright red mug standing on the black marble, Nathaniel crouched down beside the bed.

'Nice mug,' she said.

'It matches your toenails.'

'So it does,' she said, rolling over onto her side. She was going to have to leave today and she didn't want to miss a minute of looking at Nathaniel. 'What time is it?'

'Nearly eight. I would have left you sleeping but I've got a meeting with the company trustees in a few minutes and I'm not sure how long it will take.'

'Shame,' she said. 'I was going to make you porridge for breakfast.'

'I'll cancel.' He made as if to move, but she caught his arm.

'No, you're all right. I've got until two thousand and fifty-one to convert you to oatmeal.'

'I warn you, it might take that long.'

For a moment neither of them spoke. She was thinking of forty years spent sharing breakfast with Nathaniel.

He was probably thinking *help!*

'Trustees?' she prompted.

'Hastings & Hart is controlled by a family trust. Much of the profit goes to charity.'

'That explains a lot.'

'Does it?'

It explained the sense of obligation. Why he couldn't walk away.

'I found the picture Pam took of you yesterday, by the way,' he said after a moment, 'and I've made an ID card for you, Louise Braithwaite.'

'Mmm… Yes. Sorry about that, but the name Lucy Bright was given to me by the nurses in the hospital, so that's made up, too.'

'I was going to talk to you about that. I did a little research on Henshawe last night and I saw the photographs. Are you sure that your mother is a fake?'

'It's in the file.'

'All it says is that it would make a great story if they found her.'

'And it did. Not a dry eye in the house.'

'Did you like her?' he asked. 'I mean, she did abandon you.'

'Fifteen years old with a boyfriend who'd done a runner at the word pregnancy. She could have done a lot worse, Nathaniel. I'm here. But not because of her. She's a fake. Another lie generated by Rupert's PR company.'

She threw the covers back, swung her legs out of the bed, but he didn't back off.

'Okay, I liked her. More than liked.' It wouldn't have hurt so much if she'd hated her on sight. Thought her the worst mother on earth and didn't give a damn. 'We fit.' Still he didn't move. 'I loved her, okay?'

'You look like her,' he said.

'They weren't going to pick someone who didn't, were they?'

'You've got the same hair.'

'The halo or the Harpo Marx? Hair can be fixed.'

'And eyes, Lucy. Look at her eyes. You can change their colour with contacts but not their shape. And, honestly, I know that His Frogginess is capable of it, but how could he get away with it? Truly. People know her. Her history. If she was a fake, her story was a lie, don't you think someone would have sold her out to the media?'

'Aren't you going to be late for your meeting?' she said.

'Just look, okay?' Then, letting it go, 'Your employee ID is in the kitchen with a swipe card to get you through the door between the store and the apartment. There's also a store account card in the same name so that you can get anything you need. And the keypad number for the door is two five one two.'

'Two five one two,' she repeated. 'Christmas Day? I think I can remember that.'

And she wiggled her toes at him, just to show him that she'd forgiven him for bringing up her mother.

Damn. She was doing it now.

Forgetting the quotes.

'The lawyer called first thing,' Nathaniel said. 'He's spoken to the police and also issued a short statement to the press to the effect that while you're sorting out your differences with Henshawe you're staying with a friend.'

She reached up, touched his cheek. 'A very good friend.' Then, 'Nice tie, by the way.'

He was dressed for work in a crisp white shirt and the uniform pinstripes, but the tie today was candy-red.

'I've decided that it's my favourite colour.'

'Good choice.' But, despite the tie, he looked tired and she said so. 'Did you get any sleep?'

'Not much,' he admitted. 'I had a lot of thinking to do.'

'Don't tell me—I've turned your life upside down. It's a bad habit I have.'

'No, Lucy. You've turned it the right way up. And the time wasn't wasted. I've come up with a fifth option.'

'What?' She was wide awake now.

'I'm going to be late for my meeting.' He leaned forward, kissed her cheek, headed for the door.

'Nathaniel!' She leapt out of bed and went after him. Then paused, suddenly shy. 'Your tie…' She reached up to straighten it, pat it into place, keeping her eyes on the knot, but he hooked his thumb under her chin, made her look at him.

'It'll be all right. I just need to straighten a few loose ends before I put it to you.' Then, apparently forgetting all about his meeting, he caught her close, kissed her, sweet and simple, before releasing her. 'Go back to bed, Lucy.'

'I will if you'll come too.'

'You make it hard for a man to leave.'

She grinned. 'I noticed.'

'You don't really have to be an elf, you know. You can stay here. Housekeeping will come in at about ten but, apart from that, no one will disturb you.'

Too late, she was already disturbed and the condition, she feared, was terminal.

'Frank is expecting me. I can't let him down.'

'Of course you can't. He'll feed you to a troll.' He kissed her again. 'I'll see you later.' And this time he did make it to the door, where he paused to look back at her. 'Don't do anything rash, will you?'

'The rashest thing I'm going to do this morning is put maple syrup on my porridge,' she promised.

Maybe.

Diary entry: *Woken by Nathaniel, all crisp and gorgeous and ready for a hard day making dreams come true in his palace of delights. Christmas shoppers. Children. And mine? And I'm not talking about Option Five. But I will have to decide what to do today.*

Nathaniel can't be right about my mother? Can he?

The meeting began just after eight.

Nathaniel began by offering his father, his uncles, what they wanted. A Hart fully committed to the company.

Only two men in the room did not leap to accept the gesture with gratitude, relief.

Christopher's father. And his own.

He wasn't surprised.

His uncle clung vainly to the hope that one day his own son would be able to resume his place.

His father had been hurt beyond measure that he hadn't wanted to follow in his footsteps and was sure there would be a proviso.

'What do you want in return, Nathaniel?' his father asked.

'Your agreement to a proposal.' He passed around a folder as he began to talk.

* * *

Lucy retrieved her costume from the upstairs bedroom. It seemed less daunting in the daylight, with clothes heaped untidily on the bed.

She left them where they were, but picked up the rose and took it downstairs, where she tossed it, bud vase and all, into the rubbish bin tucked beneath the sink.

Start the day with a positive action. And a proper breakfast.

She sat on a stool, spooning porridge sweetened with maple syrup into her mouth, sipping her orange juice. Flipping through her messages, reading tweets, messages on Facebook. Catching up.

There was nothing more from Rupert. Not a man to waste words on a lost cause.

There were a dozen or more from the woman who claimed to be her mother. She ignored them, instead flicking through the photographs stored on her camera. The informal snaps taken when she was off guard. Zoomed in on the eyes. Compared them.

Could Nathaniel be right?

She flicked back to her messages.

Do you want to send a message?

Did she? She thumbed in a text:

Tell me the truth. Who are you? Really?

Her thumb hovered over 'send'.

Two hours later, only Nat and his father were left in the room.

'You're in love with this girl?' His father had listened to his plan, added his opinion but, now they were alone, he'd gone right to the heart of the matter.

'I only met her yesterday.'

'You're in love with her?'

'It's a good plan.'

'Can I meet her?'

'Of course. She's down in the grotto, working as an elf.'
He shrugged. 'It's a long story.'

'I've got all day.'

Lucy was sitting cross-legged on the floor, a semi-circle of
children sitting around her, totally absorbed, as she sang
them a song. They joined in the actions, roared with the
lion, hooted with the owl, quacked with the duck.

Frank, watching with a smile stretching his face, turned
as Nat joined him at the window. 'Will you just look at
that?' he said.

He needed no encouragement. 'What's going on?'

'Santa's come down with the bug and I had to send him
home. The replacement is suiting up, but there's a bit of a
backlog. Lou sent some of the elves to organise coffee for
the mothers and then rounded up the kids. I don't know
where Pam found her but I'd like half a dozen more.'

'Sorry, Frank,' Nat said. 'She's a one-off and she's mine.'
He turned to his father. 'And the answer to your question is
yes.' Love at first sight was a concept he would have denied
with his last breath. Until it happened. 'I know you'll think
I'm a fool, that it's crazy, but I'm in love with her.'

'No. I don't think you're a fool. It happens like that
sometimes. Magic happens. It was like that with your
mother and me. Just one look was all it took.'

Just one look...

Yes.

'Any chance of you bringing her home for Christmas?'

Before Nat could answer, there was a movement from
the inner sanctum and the children, almost reluctantly,
began to trickle away.

'Can we borrow your office, Frank? We need to talk
to her.'

'You're not going to take her away?'

'It's not up to me what she does; she's her own woman.' A romantic maybe, but strong, too. A woman who knew what she wanted, who never allowed anyone to control her, use her.

'Damn women's lib,' Frank muttered, stomping off to send her in.

'Nathaniel?' Lucy appeared in the doorway, hat slightly askew, curls wild, tunic rucked up behind. She tugged on it. 'Is anything wrong?'

'Nothing. My father wanted to meet you.'

'Oh.' She extended her hand. 'Hello, Mr Hart.'

'Hello, Lucy. I'm delighted to meet you. I'll leave Nathaniel to explain the situation.' He put his hand on his son's arm. 'Whatever you decide about the holiday. Your decision.'

'The holiday?' she asked when the older Hart had gone.

'We've been invited for Christmas.'

'We?'

'Us,' he said. 'It's okay. They ask me every year. They don't expect me to go.'

'Oh.'

'You sound disappointed. Sorry, but there's no way you're getting out of cooking Christmas dinner.'

'Shouldn't you check that I can cook before you commit yourself?'

'I don't actually care,' he said. Then told her about Option Five.

City Diary, London Evening Post
It was announced today that Hastings & Hart, continuing their expansion under the steady hand of Nathaniel Hart, have today acquired the Lucy

B chain from the Henshawe Corporation, who are withdrawing from the fashion business in order to concentrate on their core business.

Lucy Bright, the face of Lucy B, will be taking a more hands-on role in the business and is joining Hastings & Hart in January as a director of the Lucy B division with responsibility for fair trade development.

Rupert Henshawe is relinquishing the chairmanship of the Henshawe Corporation with immediate effect. Shares in the company were down in trading.

Slight wobble, tweeps, but the frog has been vanquished and LucyB is back and on target. Thanks for all the support.
LucyB, Fri 3 Dec 10:14

Lucy flicked through her followers, picking out the ones that were missing. Jenpb was gone. A couple of others. But *WelshWitch* was cheering her on and, on an impulse, she sent her a direct message. Something only she could read.

WelshWitch Want to meet for lunch? DM me.
Fri 3 Dec 10:16

There was just one more thing to do. She scrolled through the numbers in her phonebook and hit 'dial'.

'Lucy?'

'Mum...'

And then they were both crying.

* * *

Friday, 24th December
Appointments
09:30 Hair and stuff
11:00 Meeting with Marji from Celebrity
12:30 Lunch (with my mum!)
17:00 Reception for trustees in boardroom
20:00 Dinner in Garden Restaurant to celebrate
Hastings & Hart takeover of Lucy B launch

'Happy?' Nat said as they returned to the apartment after a Christmas Eve dinner for family and friends in the Garden Restaurant on the seventh floor—a celebration that her mother had been part of, too. Because, while Rupert Henshawe's ability to deceive had gone as far as pretending that he'd looked for her, she was the one who'd come forward when she'd read the story in the newspaper.

'Blissful,' she assured him. 'But what about you?' she asked, hooking her arm in his. 'Are you really prepared to let go of your career in architecture?'

'Says my biggest critic.'

'No. This building is amazing. The apartment is amazing. It just needs a little internal glow.'

He paused at the entrance, turned to her.

'You give it that, Lucy. It means light, doesn't it. Lucy?'

She nodded.

'Well, that's what you are. A light shining into all the dark places. You've lit up my life. Warmed my heart—'

'Nathaniel…'

'It's too soon to say this, you're going to think me a fool and, no, it's nothing to do with making you a director of Lucy B. You've earned that with your heart.'

'I'm terrified I'll get it wrong.'

'Terror is the default setting when you're at the top. But

you're not on your own.' He reached out to her hand. 'Never on your own.'

Her fingers wrapped around his and he felt the tension slide away as it always did when she was close. 'You are going to be wonderful. My father said so and he's no push-over for a pretty face.'

'I like your dad. And your mother. It was so kind of them to invite my mum for Christmas, too.'

'They knew that, wherever she was, you'd want to be, Lucy. That, wherever you were, I'd want to be, too.'

'I owe you a Christmas dinner,' she said, looking up. 'I guess that takes us to two thousand and fifty-two—'

'You think I'm letting you go that easily?' he growled. 'What I'm trying to say is that this is not a get-your-kit-off line. I love you. I loved you from the moment I first saw you.' With his other hand he reached out and touched her cheek, very gently, almost afraid that she would disappear under his touch. 'Just saying. You don't have to do a thing about it.'

'But, if I wanted to get my kit off, that would be all right?' she asked seriously. Looking up at him with those green-gold eyes, soft, filled with warmth, joy, happiness.

He swallowed. 'Your call.' Then, before she could move, 'But maybe you want to think about that. Give yourself some time.'

'And if I don't?'

'Then you can forget about flat-hunting. You won't be going anywhere.'

'If I stay here, I'll make changes,' she warned.

'You already have.' Pop music on the radio first thing in the morning. Pots of early jonquils brightening every surface. Laughter everywhere.

'Phooey. That's nothing. If I stay, I warn you, I'll want to paint the walls primrose-yellow.'

'I'll help you.'

'Hang pictures everywhere.'

'I've got a hammer.'

'Get a kitten.'

'Only one?' he asked.

'Well, they do get lonely without their brothers and sisters,' she said, a glint of mischief in her eyes. 'Two would be better.'

'Bring the whole damn litter.'

Her smile deepened momentarily and then, suddenly, she was serious. 'There's one more thing.'

'You want your mother to live with us?'

'You'd do that for me?' she asked. Then, shaking her head, she let him off the hook. 'It's not that. I want you to build the house in Cornwall.'

'For you—'

'No, Nathaniel; not for me. For you.' And, as if she knew that was the most difficult thing she'd asked, she lifted herself onto her toes and, coiling her arms around his neck, she kissed him. Giving him her courage, her strength, all her love.

There was no need. She'd been giving him that since the day she'd stumbled in front of him on the stairs. In that moment the fairy tale had changed from Cinderella to something entirely new. She'd brought the sleeping Beast back to life with a kiss, made him whole again. But he had one condition of his own.

'It's a house for a family, Lucy. I'll build it if you'll help me fill it.'

'Fill it?'

'With kittens, puppies, your mother. Our children.' There was a still moment when the world seemed to hold its breath. 'I love you, Lucy Bright. Will you marry me?'

'I...'

'It's a big decision. You'll need time to think about it.'

'Yes…' For a moment the world seemed to hang on its axis. Then she said, 'I've thought about it.' And, reaching for the single button holding together the green-gold silk Lucy B jacket that she was wearing, 'How soon can you get that door open?'

Lucy hadn't got it free when he pushed the door open, but this time he was the one who came to a shocked halt.

'A little extra glow,' she said as he took in the eight-foot Christmas tree laden with toys and candy canes and painted glass balls. A replica of the one in the grotto. Or had she just had it shifted? Frank would do anything for her.

There were swathes of greenery, a forest of plants sparkling with tiny white lights. Thick red pillar candles.

'I used my Louise Braithwaite store card,' she said. 'This is your Christmas gift from the elf.'

Then she let her jacket slip to the floor, raised her arms.

'But this one is from me. With all my heart, Nathaniel. All my love. All you have to do is unwrap it and enjoy.'

Lucy gazed at the familiar view. The rugged landscape, the deep blue of the distant sea. Familiar but different. And she smiled.

These days, when they bumped down the track in the big black Range Rover, the rocky ledge was topped by a long, low house that appeared to grow out of it. That over the years had become so much part of the landscape that it deceived the eye. The glass wall facing the sea a perfect reflection of the land. The rock and stone indivisible. One. Like the two of them.

Nathaniel turned to the rear. 'Out you get, boys. Let's get the car unloaded.' Then, as their two sturdy lads scrambled out, whooping to be free, eager to get at the sand, the sea, he reached across, laid his hand across her expanding waist, his eyes more silver than grey. 'Okay?'

'Absolutely. Our little girl and I will sit here and enjoy the view while you unload.'

'You're facing the house,' he pointed out.

'I know. It's my favourite view in all the world.' The house that he had designed for himself, built for her. More beloved than any palace. Just as he was so much more than any Prince Charming. Her rock. Her partner. Her beloved husband. The father of her children. A man at peace with life, with himself.

'Can we pitch the tent, Daddy?'

'I want to build a den.'

'What do you want, Lucy B?' Nathaniel asked, taking her hand, lifting it to his lips.

'I've got everything I ever wanted,' she said. 'How about you?'

'I have you, Lucy. Everything else follows from that,' he said, leaning across to kiss her.

Coming Next Month

Available December 7, 2010

REQUEST YOUR FREE BOOKS!
2 FREE NOVELS PLUS 2
FREE GIFTS!

 HARLEQUIN® *Romance®*

From the Heart, For the Heart

YES! Please send me 2 FREE Harlequin® Romance novels and my 2 FREE gifts (gifts are worth about $10). After receiving them, if I don't wish to receive any more books, I can return the shipping statement marked "cancel". If I don't cancel, I will receive 6 brand-new novels every month and be billed just $3.84 per book in the U.S. or $4.24 per book in Canada. That's a savings of 15% off the cover price! It's quite a bargain! Shipping and handling is just 50¢ per book.* I understand that accepting the 2 free books and gifts places me under no obligation to buy anything. I can always return a shipment and cancel at any time. Even if I never buy another book from Harlequin, the two free books and gifts are mine to keep forever.

116/316 HDN E7T2

Name _____ (PLEASE PRINT)

Address _____ Apt. #

City _____ State/Prov. _____ Zip/Postal Code

Signature (if under 18, a parent or guardian must sign)

Mail to the **Harlequin Reader Service:**
IN U.S.A.: P.O. Box 1867, Buffalo, NY 14240-1867
IN CANADA: P.O. Box 609, Fort Erie, Ontario L2A 5X3

Not valid for current subscribers to Harlequin Romance books.

**Are you a subscriber to Harlequin Romance books
and want to receive the larger-print edition?
Call 1-800-873-8635 or visit www.ReaderService.com.**

* Terms and prices subject to change without notice. Prices do not include applicable taxes. Sales tax applicable in N.Y. Canadian residents will be charged applicable provincial taxes and GST. Offer not valid in Quebec. This offer is limited to one order per household. All orders subject to approval. Credit or debit balances in a customer's account(s) may be offset by any other outstanding balance owed by or to the customer. Please allow 4 to 6 weeks for delivery. Offer available while quantities last.

Your Privacy: Harlequin Books is committed to protecting your privacy. Our Privacy Policy is available online at www.ReaderService.com or upon request from the Reader Service. From time to time we make our lists of customers available to reputable third parties who may have a product or service of interest to you. If you would prefer we not share your name and address, please check here. ☐

Help us get it right—We strive for accurate, respectful and relevant communications. To clarify or modify your communication preferences, visit us at www.ReaderService.com/consumerschoice.

HR10R2

HARLEQUIN®

A Romance

FOR EVERY MOOD™

Spotlight on

Classic

Quintessential, modern love stories
that are romance at its finest.

See the next page
to enjoy a sneak peek from
the Harlequin® Romance series.

See below for a sneak peek from our classic
Harlequin® Romance® line.

Introducing DADDY BY CHRISTMAS by Patricia Thayer.

MIA caught sight of Jarrett when he walked into the open lobby. It was hard not to notice the man. In a charcoal business suit with a crisp white shirt and striped tie covered by a dark trench coat, he looked more Wall Street than small-town Colorado.

Mia couldn't blame him for keeping his distance. He was probably tired of taking care of her.

Besides, why would a man like Jarrett McKane be interested in her? Why would he want to take on a woman expecting a baby? Yet he'd done so many things for her. He'd been there when she'd needed him most. How could she not care about a man like that?

Heart pounding in her ears, she walked up behind him. Jarrett turned to face her. "Did you get enough sleep last night?"

"Yes, thanks to you," she said, wondering if he'd thought about their kiss. Her gaze went to his mouth, then she quickly glanced away. "And thank you for not bringing up my meltdown."

Jarrett couldn't stop looking at Mia. Blue was definitely her color, bringing out the richness of her eyes.

"What meltdown?" he said, trying hard to focus on what she was saying. "You were just exhausted from lack of sleep and worried about your baby."

He couldn't help remembering how, during the night, he'd kept going in to watch her sleep. How strange was that? "I hope you got enough rest."

She nodded. "Plenty. And you're a good neighbor for

coming to my rescue."

He tensed. Neighbor? *What neighbor kisses you like I did?* "That's me, just the full-service landlord," he said, trying to keep the sarcasm out of his voice. He started to leave, but she put her hand on his arm.

"Jarrett, what I meant was you went beyond helping me." Her eyes searched his face. "I've asked far too much of you."

"Did you hear me complain?"

She shook her head. "You should. I feel like I've taken advantage."

"Like I said, I haven't minded."

"And I'm grateful for everything…"

Grasping her hand on his arm, Jarrett leaned forward. The memory of last night's kiss had him aching for another. "I didn't do it for your gratitude, Mia."

Gorgeous tycoon Jarrett McKane has never believed in Christmas—but he can't help being drawn to soon-to-be-mom Mia Saunders! Christmases past were spent alone…and now Jarrett may just have a fairy-tale ending for all his Christmases future!

Available December 2010, only from Harlequin® Romance®.

HREXP1210

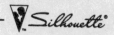

SPECIAL EDITION

USA TODAY BESTSELLING AUTHOR

MARIE FERRARELLA

BRINGS YOU ANOTHER
HEARTWARMING STORY FROM

When Lilli McCall disappeared on him
after he proposed, Kullen Manetti swore
never to fall in love again. Eight years later
Lilli is back in his life, threatening to break
down all the walls he's put up to
safeguard his heart.

UNWRAPPING
THE PLAYBOY

*Available December
wherever books are sold.*